About the Author

John Fuller obtained a first-class honours degree in chemical engineering from Imperial College. He worked for three years for BP as a research engineer in the fields of combustion and two-phase flow. He then joined a firm of consulting scientists and engineers, which specialises in the investigation of fires and explosions for insurance companies. John was a partner for twenty years and is now retired. He lives with his wife in Hampshire and indulges his hobbies of watercolour painting, bird-watching and horse-racing.

Fired

To Caroline,
Best wishes,
from John

John Fuller

John Fuller

Fired

Olympia Publishers
London

www.olympiapublishers.com
OLYMPIA PAPERBACK EDITION

A CIP catalogue record for this title is
available from the British Library.

ISBN: 978-1-83543-151-1

First Published in 2025

Olympia Publishers
Tallis House
2 Tallis Street
London
EC4Y 0AB

Printed in Great Britain

Dedication

This book is dedicated to my family, friends and former colleagues, without whom this book would not have been possible.

Chapter 1

It was a glassware Armageddon. The cheap glass vases and ornaments, which had originally been contained in palletised cardboard boxes stored on parallel rows of Dexion racking, were lying broken in deep piles in the warehouse aisles, the fire having almost completely destroyed the boxes and the pallets. Fragments of corrugated cement sheeting from the warehouse single-skin roof, which had shattered and collapsed in the fire, were strewn amongst the broken glass; and isolated snakes of smoke were rising up from smoulders still progressing in the piles. The fire had been so intense that the facing internal brick walls of the integral, two-storey front office had cracked thereby allowing smoke to progress into the offices and deposit as thick soot.

There was no discernible variation in the degree of damage in the warehouse, which was a real problem for me as I had been instructed to investigate the cause of the fire for the insurers of the contents and business interruption losses. More precisely, Millans, Chartered Loss Adjusters, who were professional claims handlers appointed by the insurers, had instructed Jacobs, Forensic Scientists and Engineers, to investigate the cause of the fire for insurers; and I, James Gabriel, a partner in Jacobs, had taken on the case. As was usual and often essential for a forensic investigation, insurers had asked for an immediate attendance, the fire having occurred on the previous evening, Tuesday, 15 November 2022. Accordingly, within ten minutes of taking the instruction, I was travelling with my kit-bag in a taxi along the A13 from Jacobs' converted public house office located off Brick Lane in the City of London.

I spent the journey more than a little annoyed. When the Millans' loss adjuster, Sheena Narni, a long-standing client, had rang in with the instruction, only myself and Marty Adair, Jacobs' managing partner, were available to take the instruction, the remaining four partners and eight associates being out of the office investigating other cases. Marty, tall, fair-haired and avuncular, oozed charm, particularly with clients he had known for many years, and since he had been made managing partner three years ago, he had specialised in taking on large cases with long deadlines. He maintained that his management duties made it difficult for him to take on cases that required immediate attendance.

Selena, our chic, self-contained receptionist, who was also Marty's secretary, had asked me to take Sheena's call, and after quickly scribbling Sheena's instructions, I, who was juggling with numerous urgent cases, went into Marty's second-floor office to ask whether he could deal with the case. Selena was also in Marty's office on Marty's side of his desk, and they both jumped slightly when I entered, with Selena then looking down at an apparently empty part of the desktop and Marty immediately picking up a sheet of paper and looking at it whilst hiding it from my view. My already metaphorically raised eyebrows were heightened when I noticed – due to the low, winter sun shining brightly through the office window behind Marty and partly through the paper – that the hidden text was actually in the form of a spreadsheet, which was upside down.

"Sorry, James," Marty drawled before I said anything, "I won't be able to deal with that case. Selena and I have to sort out the management accounts."

Selena, still breathless from having run upstairs, flushed slightly and tilted her head towards the upside-down spreadsheet.

"I didn't know you could read minds," I replied drily to a blank-faced Marty. I decided not to add that it was the middle of the month so I could not see why the management accounts were so urgent. Instead, I asked Selena to ring for a taxi whilst I called the insured to make arrangements to attend the scene. I then left the office focused on infinity.

Sheena Narni, petite, efficient and worried, blinked at the acrid smoke as she stood with me on top of the debris in one of the warehouse aisles.

"I know it is a difficult one, James, but there is pressure from insurers because it is a £1 million contents and business interruption claim and preliminary indications are that Dagenham Glass has been in decline for some years. Also" – Sheena hesitated – "Markham is involved, and he's appointed Degsy."

I made a physical effort not to flinch. Harry Markham was a one-man-band loss assessor, who offered to represent people who had suffered an insurance loss, the insured signing a contract with the assessor agreeing that the assessor received a percentage of the payout made by the insurers. By way of comparison, chartered loss adjusters, like Sheena, were paid an hourly rate by insurers, regardless of the outcome of a claim. Often following a large fire, several loss assessor companies would attend the scene offering their services to the insured.

"An experienced claims professional who assists victims of fire, water leaks and storm damage in obtaining the best payout from insurers," according to Markham's business card.

"An odious, slippery rat," according to Sheena Narni who, like me, had encountered Markham numerous times during the three years that he had been loss assessing. As if on cue, Markham emerged from the internal doorway of the office block wearing a fur-collared overcoat, a ridiculous pork-pie hat and a slight, sneering smile on his small but pinched face. A pencil moustache completed the spiv look, and as on previous meetings, I wondered how intentional this was. A short, rotund man with thinning, grey hair accompanied Markham.

"James," said Sheena, as Markham and his companion approached, "can I introduce Ronnie Stanshaw, the owner of Dagenham Glass? You know Harry Markham."

Ronnie Stanshaw held out a hand which I shook.

"This is that smart-alec investigator I was telling you about," volunteered Markham before Mr Stanshaw could speak. Not short of confidence, Markham continued in his nasal, patronising voice, "As you can see, Gabriel, this is a straightforward case. It's obviously one of the lights."

"I didn't know you had any fire investigation expertise," I replied in a deliberately puzzled tone.

Markham's eyes flashed, and his nostrils flared, whilst Mr Stanshaw coughed nervously. Markham smoothly changed gear. "I've appointed a proper fire investigator," Markham said smirking, "someone with practical fire brigade experience…" He paused for dramatic effect "Derek Isaac."

Much to Markham's annoyance, my only physical reaction was a raised eyebrow. "It's not clear to me how thirty years' experience of squirting water into burning buildings is helpful in the scientific investigation of fires, but perhaps he can enlighten us," I continued, glancing to the internal doorway of the office block, as Markham's jaw dropped.

Derek aka 'Degsy' Isaac, overweight, overconfident and overly slicked-back hair had arrived at the doorway shortly after Markham and Mr Stanshaw but had remained there staring bleakly around the warehouse. Seeing us looking at him, he slowly made his way towards us. "Afternoon," he reluctantly grunted when I caught his eye.

"Afternoon, Derek," I replied, deliberately cheerful. "I understand you have a theory that this fire was caused by the lights."

"It's not a theory," he replied quickly. "It's quite clear to anyone who knows about fire investigation."

"Really?" I said. "What is the evidence, given that the remains of the fluorescent lights have collapsed and are mostly buried beneath the debris?"

"I have interviewed Mr Stanshaw's son, Warren, the general manager, who was last to leave yesterday, and he told me that a light had been left on in the warehouse, as usual, to deter intruders. A faulty fluorescent light producing hot debris, which falls and ignites combustible material is a well-known cause of fires... and there is no other plausible cause," Isaac asserted, closing his eyes learnedly.

"How does leaving a light on in the warehouse deter an intruder?" I asked. "It is unlikely an intruder would see the light through the skylights as the roof is high and has a shallow slope. Surely it would be better to leave one of the lights on in one of the office blocks' front offices."

Markham, Isaac and Mr Stanshaw barely breathed as the cogs whirled between their ears.

"What are you saying?" was the eventual, slightly threatening offering from Markham.

"As always, I am saying exactly what I am thinking," I said.

"Also," I continued, turning to Isaac, "all the warehouse light switches, which are next to the internal door, have largely survived the fire but they are all immovable, because the fire charred them in position... the 'off' position."

Isaac's jaw muscles bunched. "Sometimes light switches are installed upside down," he said.

"But you said a light was left switched on," I said, emphasising the 'a', "so surely one switch should be in a different position to the others, whereas, they are all in the same position."

Isaac glanced towards the internal doorway, but as it was about 10 metres away, the switch positions could not be seen from where we were standing.

"Rather than stand here and speculate," Isaac said snorting, "I think we should electrically check the switches."

"Let's do that then," I said, "after which, I would like to interview Warren Stanshaw."

"I will need to be present during any interview," said Isaac pompously.

"Fine, where is Warren?"

"He's just speaking to Michael, one of our van drivers, who left with us just before the fire yesterday," said Ronnie Stanshaw.

"So three of you left together then, not just Warren, which is what I thought you had said," I queried, turning to Isaac.

"Michael works in the warehouse in the afternoon making up the following day's deliveries, and he was last to leave the warehouse through the internal door," said Ronnie Stanshaw. "He then came upstairs and left copies of the delivery notes on the accounts clerk's desk. Warren and I chatted with him upstairs then we all went downstairs to the reception area. Michael and I left and chatted outside whilst Warren set the alarm in the reception area," said Mr Stanshaw.

"That's why the van driver's here," said Isaac. "We've got him to come in so he can confirm all this."

"Thank you," I said and added. "It's unusual for you to be so thoughtful."

I noticed Markham glance at Isaac who said, "Shall we look at these light switches?"

Isaac and I, both wearing overalls, hard hats and steel-capped boots, made our way to the internal door and placed our kit-bags on the ground. Sheena, Markham and Mr Stanshaw followed us.

Mr Stanshaw looked at the light switches somewhat grim-faced and said, "How long will you be? Only Michael can't hang around as he's helping us set up again in a temporary building."

"We'll only be a few minutes checking these switches," I said.

"Okay," said Markham, "Mr Stanshaw and I will get Warren and Michael ready to speak to you in the large, ground-floor meeting room, which is probably the cleanest. Sheena, I just want to have a private word with Mr Stanshaw, then we can start on stock estimates."

Markham then ushered Mr Stanshaw into the office block, leaving a stony-faced Sheena to watch Isaac and I remove the light switch assembly from its wall recess with the assistance of a screwdriver. As was usual, the internal components of the light switches had been protected from severe fire attack by their front mounting plate and the surrounding wall structure, and by applying the probes of a portable electrical continuity tester across the terminations of the switches, we quickly established that all the switches were in the off position.

"This only means the light assemblies couldn't have caused the fire," said Isaac, again closing his eyes. "Electrical faults can still occur on lighting circuits even if the light switches are off because there is always a live supply up to the junction boxes between the light switches and the light assemblies."

"But all the junction boxes and the wiring conduit are steel, which as usual, has survived the fire," I said, deliberately pointing to the nearest collapsed conduit and junction box that were hanging from part of the RSJ frame of the warehouse, "so even if an electrical fault had occurred, it couldn't have initiated a fire external to the conduit. You agree with that, don't you, Georgie?" I continued, looking at a slim, fair-haired young woman with pursed lips who had appeared at the internal doorway: Georgie O'Brien of Willoughbys, the second largest fire and explosion investigators in the country, based in Doncaster and Milton Keynes, and Jacobs' main rivals. Georgie herself was much better than Isaac as a fire investigator but had an aversion to evidence that didn't suit her client's interests.

"Good afternoon, James," said Georgie in her quiet voice. "I am appointed by the insurers of the landlord. and I can assure you that the electrical circuits were tested less than a year ago. I've got copies of the certificates."

"And copies for us no doubt," I said with a little emphasis.

"Of course," she replied with only slightly affected offence.

"There you are then, Derek," I said, continuing determinedly with my cheerfulness, "a cause involving the lighting circuits doesn't seem to be a very good candidate at all as a cause of the fire."

Isaac's mouth twisted unhappily. "I think we should speak to Warren," he said. "He's been kept waiting for us far too long," seemingly forgetting it was his idea to check the light switches.

Sheena, Georgie, Isaac and I made our way into the office block, with Isaac leading the way. As we approached the ground-floor meeting room, the sounds of a heated exchange became evident, with Ronnie Stanshaw's raised voice particularly noticeable, but Isaac coughed loudly as he opened the office door and the noise ceased instantly.

When we entered, a red-faced Ronnie Stanshaw was breathing heavily and standing over and to one side of a bespectacled, sweating, younger version of himself who was sitting at one end of a boardroom table. Markham was standing with his hands partly raised in a calming gesture on the other side of the younger version of Mr Stanshaw, but Markham smoothly moved his hands to an introductory flourish and shamelessly switching to first-name charm said, "James, this is Ronnie's son, Warren."

"I think there's been a misunderstanding about the lights," blurted out Warren, skipping any introductory pleasantries. "I thought a light had been left switched on in the warehouse but obviously it hadn't."

"Why did you think that? You weren't in the warehouse," I replied.

"No, but Michael knew he had to leave a warehouse light on, which is why I told Mr Isaac he would have left a light on."

"Were you working in the warehouse at any time yesterday?" I asked.

"No, I was working in the offices all day with Dad and the other office staff."

"Did any of them go into the warehouse?"

"No."

"What time did the other office staff leave?" I asked.

"About half past four, as usual," replied Warren.

"What other electrical equipment is there in the warehouse other than the lights?" asked Georgie.

"None," said Warren, "apart from the intruder alarm and fire alarm systems."

"Could you describe the intruder alarm system, please?" asked Georgie.

"I'll describe it," said Ronnie Stanshaw. "There are passive infrared – that's PIR – movement detectors positioned on the walls of the warehouse and directed along each aisle. There are also PIRs in the offices and contacts on the external doors. The alarm control box is in a cupboard in the reception area, and the system is monitored by the alarm company."

"Is it a wireless system?" I asked.

"No. Wiring connects the PIRs and contacts to the alarm control box," said Ronnie.

"And the fire alarm system?" asked Georgie.

"There are break glass cells throughout the building," said Ronnie.

"No heat or smoke detectors?" asked Georgie.

"No," said Ronnie.

"Any CCTV cameras?" asked Georgie.

"No," said Ronnie.

"Have there been any electrical problems?" asked Georgie.

"No," said Ronnie, "and the electrical circuits are checked regularly, as you are aware."

"Does anyone smoke?" I asked.

"Smoking is illegal in commercial premises, as you should know," said Markham.

"That doesn't answer the question," I said. "I would like to know if anyone smokes."

"No one smokes," said Ronnie.

"Do you use a fork-lift truck to move the stock?" asked Georgie.

"Yes, it's parked in the warehouse access bay," said Ronnie.

"How is it powered?" I asked.

"Propane gas cylinder," said Ronnie, "but it wasn't that; the fire didn't get into the access bay, and the fork-lift truck is only covered in soot."

"So, what time did Michael leave the warehouse via the internal door... without leaving a light switched on?" I asked.

"He came up to the upstairs office at about ten to five," said Ronnie Stanshaw.

"And left the delivery notes on the accounts clerk's desk?" I asked.

"Mr Stanshaw has already told you this," said Markham, exasperatedly.

"Georgie wasn't here when Mr Stanshaw told me that, and she needs to know," I said. "You all then went straight down to the reception area?" I asked.

"We actually chatted with Michael in the office for a short time," said Ronnie. "Michael and his wife have just had their first baby, and we were asking Michael how the baby was getting on."

"Okay, keep going for Georgie's benefit."

"Well, we all then went down to reception, and Michael and I went outside and continued chatting whilst Warren set the alarm," said Ronnie Stanshaw.

"There were no problems setting the alarm?" I asked, turning to Warren Stanshaw.

"No, no problems," said Warren, hesitating slightly.

"Then you went straight outside?" I asked.

"Yes."

"How long does it take to walk from the alarm control box to the external reception doors?"

"About five seconds, and you have to be quick otherwise the

alarm will go off if you haven't gone outside and closed the external door within thirty seconds of setting the alarm."

"Is the alarm operated by a keypad?"

"No, there is a key which we leave in the control box."

"How do you know that the alarm has actually set?"

"When you turn the key on, a green light appears on the control box and there is a beeping noise to warn you to get out."

"And you observed both of those?"

"Yes."

"Okay. So, once you got outside, what happened?"

"I said good night to Michael who then got into his van and drove off. Dad and I turned to get into Dad's car, and just as we were getting in, a woman who was outside the double-glazing unit opposite us, shouted to us that flames were coming from our warehouse roof."

"Who was this woman?"

"I don't know, but she was one of the double-glazing people because she was wearing one of their fleeces."

"Before we go any further, what time was this?"

"I don't know; sometime after five. I didn't actually look at my watch when the woman told us about the fire," said Warren, feeling pleased with himself at apparently scoring a point in the interview.

"What did you do when she alerted you to the fire?" I asked, ignoring his smug expression.

"I got in the car and drove off... to fetch Michael," said Warren, looking slightly sheepish.

"Why?" I asked, puzzled.

"To tell him about the fire," said Warren, slightly challengingly.

"Why do you think?" said Markham, irritated.

"What did you do, Mr Stanshaw?" asked Georgie, frowning and turning to Ronnie Stanshaw.

"I went over to the woman then looked back to the warehouse," said Ronnie. "I saw flames coming from the rear left side of the warehouse roof."

"When was someone last in the rear left side of the warehouse?" I asked.

"Possibly not for a week or so; we keep stock that is rarely purchased in that area," said Ronnie Stanshaw.

"Are there any other warehouse staff?" I asked.

"No, only Michael, and he only works in the warehouse in the afternoon making up the deliveries for the next day. He makes deliveries in the morning. There are two other van drivers, but they only collect their deliveries from the warehouse access bay in the morning then spend the day making deliveries."

"Do those two drivers return to the warehouse after making their deliveries?" I asked.

"No, they just go home; they are allowed to drive their empty vans between their homes and the warehouse," said Ronnie Stanshaw.

"After you saw the flames coming from the roof, what did you do?" I asked Ronnie Stanshaw.

"I started to call the fire brigade on my mobile, but the woman said she had already called them, so I ran back towards our building. As I did so, our intruder alarm started sounding," said Ronnie, "but I kept going, unlocked the reception door, went into the reception, switched on the lights, grabbed a fire extinguisher, went along the corridor and opened the internal warehouse door. I was going to try to fight the fire but when I looked into the warehouse, I could see the fire was too large, so I came back outside. The woman had actually come into the building and was screaming down the corridor for me to come out."

"How long did it take for the fire brigade to arrive?" I asked.

"Less than ten minutes, but the fire was going like a train by then, so they couldn't do anything to stop it," said Ronnie Stanshaw.

"Had you returned with Michael before the fire brigade arrived?" I asked Warren.

"I had returned but not with Michael. I was stuck at the junction with the main road because of rush-hour traffic coming both ways, and by the time I had turned right, he had disappeared so I came back," said Warren.

"Why didn't you just call him on his mobile?" I asked.

"I don't know…" said Warren. "I think that because of the fire I wasn't thinking straight… and I decided to just come back and help Dad."

"What did the fire brigade do?" I asked.

"By the time they arrived, the fire was coming from almost all of the roof," said Ronnie Stanshaw. "They connected up their hoses and poured water into the building over the walls. I also unlocked the warehouse access bay door so the fire brigade could raise it and put water in through there. It took over two hours to dampen the fire down."

"Where is Michael now?" I asked.

"We asked him to go and wait outside just before you arrived," said Markham.

"I think we can speak to him now," I said.

Ronnie Stanshaw called Michael on his mobile phone, and after a short time, Michael, a thin, nervous, red-haired young man entered the room and nodded deferentially to Ronnie Stanshaw.

"Sorry for keeping you waiting, Michael," said Markham,

pleasantly. "These insurance investigators would like to ask you some questions about when you left with Warren yesterday."

"Before we get to that," I said, "can you tell me where you were working in the warehouse on the afternoon of the fire and what you were doing?" I asked.

"I was working in the centre and on the right-hand side and was taking stock from the shelves, making up the deliveries for the vans to pick up the next day... today," said Michael.

"Did you work in the left side of the warehouse?" I asked.

"No, there was no stock in that area for the deliveries I was making up," said Michael.

"You used the fork-lift truck to make up the deliveries?" asked Georgie.

"Yes."

"And were there any problems with the truck?" asked Georgie.

"No, it worked fine as usual."

"Did you leave it on charge?" asked Georgie.

"No, I parked it next to the charger in the access bay, but I didn't connect it to the charger. It had been charged on the previous day and still had plenty of charge."

"Were there any problems with the warehouse lights?" asked Georgie. "Were any flashing?"

"No, no problems. There was no flashing."

"Did you switch off the lights when you left?" I asked.

"Well," said Michael, "just before I went outside to wait my turn to be interviewed, Mr Stanshaw told me that I had switched them all off, but I thought I had left one light switched on."

"Which is what you have been doing for years?" I said.

"Well, no," said Michael, "Warren only asked me to start leaving one of the lights on about a month ago. I did forget a

23

couple of times the first week, but after that, I remembered. I suppose I must have forgotten again yesterday."

"What prompted you to ask Michael to leave the lights switched on?" I asked, turning to Warren.

"For God's sake, he's already told you: to deter intruders," said Markham, raising his voice.

"That's not the point," I said quietly. "I want to know what happened a month ago that resulted in Warren giving an instruction to Michael to leave a light on in the warehouse. Why wasn't that instruction given six months ago or six years ago?"

Warren remained silent and blinked furiously, but after a short pause, Ronnie Stanshaw said, "We were just thinking about the large amount of stock in the warehouse, and we thought it would be safer to leave a strip of lights on."

"Are you a smoker?" I asked Michael.

"No, I've never smoked," said Michael.

"Were there any unusual smells in the warehouse whilst you were working there yesterday afternoon?" I asked.

"No, no odd smells."

"Were there any visitors to the warehouse during the afternoon?" asked Georgie.

"No."

"What time did you leave the warehouse?" I asked.

"Warren's already told you that," said Markham, shaking his head.

"Warren also told me that he couldn't remember what time he was alerted to the fire, so I would like Michael's recollections as to when he left the warehouse," I said.

"It was about ten to five," said Michael.

Markham smiled, still shaking his head.

"Then what did you do?" I asked, prompting more

headshaking from Markham.

"I took the delivery paperwork up to accounts and made some notes for the accounts staff," said Michael. "Mr Stanshaw and Warren were in the office, and Mr Stanshaw asked about Charlie... My wife and I have just had our first baby." Michael smiled naturally when he thought of his family.

"Congratulations," I said, also smiling. "Just keep going with what happened."

"Okay, so after chatting for a few minutes, we all went downstairs to reception. Me and Mr Stanshaw went outside whilst Warren set the alarm."

"You saw Warren set the alarm?" I asked.

"Completely unacceptable," commented Markham.

"No, it's not," I said. "People make mistakes. Michael thought he had left a light switched on in the warehouse, but no lights were actually left switched on. Warren might be mistaken that he switched the alarm on, so it's entirely correct for me to ask Michael if he saw Warren set the alarm."

"I did actually see Warren set the alarm," said Michael.

"From outside?" I said.

"You're priceless, you are," said Markham. "You must've noticed the reception has large windows and that the reception door is glazed."

"I'd like Michael to answer," I said.

"There's no problem," said Michael. "I was looking into the reception, and I did see Warren set the alarm."

"When I arrived this afternoon," I said, "I noticed a small cupboard labelled 'Alarm' – which I assume contains the intruder alarm control box – on a side wall in the reception area and that the cupboard door opened out towards the reception door, so surely when you looked into the reception you could only have

25

seen Warren reach into the cupboard. You couldn't have seen him set the alarm."

"You should go on the stage," said Markham, "you'd make a good comedian. If he reaches into the cupboard, he's going to set the alarm. Why wouldn't he?"

"Anyway," Markham continued triumphantly, "we know the alarm was set because it started sounding shortly after the fire was discovered."

"Really," I said with emphasis, "did you hear the beeping noise when you saw Warren reach into the cupboard containing the alarm control box?" I asked, turning to Michael.

"No, but I don't think you can hear it outside anyway; it's not that loud," said Michael.

"I did set the alarm," said Warren.

"What happened after Warren set the alarm?" I asked Michael.

"You already know this," snapped Markham.

"You must let him answer," I said.

"Well, Warren switched off the lights, came outside and locked the reception door. Mr Stanshaw was still chatting to me about Charlie, but after Warren came out, he stopped talking, and I got in my van and drove off."

"What time was that?" I asked.

"Just after five," said Michael.

"When you got to the junction with the main road, did you have to wait?" I asked.

"No, I was able to turn right straight away," said Michael.

"Okay, thank you, Michael," I said. "Has anyone else got any questions?"

There were no more questions, so we thanked Michael again and he left the room.

"I would like to carry out a detailed inspection of the building, and as there is not much daylight left, I will start now and return tomorrow," I said. "No doubt Georgie and Derek will want to carry out their inspections with me?"

"Yes," said Georgie.

"I will, of course, give you whatever assistance you require," said Isaac, cack-handedly attempting to acquire some moral high ground.

"Perhaps we can look at the intruder alarm control box first," I said.

Sheena, who along with me had been making notes during the interviews said, "Should we make a start on the stock-take, Harry?"

"I'd like to see the alarm control box first," said Markham, tilting his head and looking at me.

We all trooped along to the reception area, and Warren unlocked the cupboard containing the alarm control box. The cupboard door was opened, and Markham stood on the reception window side of it, no doubt noticing that in the open position, the cupboard door did prevent someone outside the building from viewing the actions of someone reaching into the cupboard. Markham snorted slightly then tried to look over the shoulders of Georgie, Isaac and me as we looked into the cupboard.

"It's clear the key was in the set position," said Isaac with his eyelids in the fully closed, learned position.

The key certainly was in the set position, and further, the soot, which had penetrated the cupboard and deposited on the alarm control box and the key, had not been disturbed since the fire, such disturbance being expected if the key had been switched to the on position after the fire. It followed that the key was in the set position at the time of the fire.

A Cheshire cat would have been proud of the smile on Markham's face. "Any more questions?" he said, looking at me.

"This alarm box is a basic design that can't be interrogated, so I would like the intruder alarm company details and a letter from Dagenham Glass providing me with authority to ask the alarm company for a technical specification for the alarm system and a copy of the alarm record for the premises," I replied.

"You're flapping now," sneered Markham.

"The alarm record should show, which particular alarm circuit activated first, and that information could indicate the area of the warehouse where the fire started," I said. "Also, if the alarm was set, the set time will have been recorded."

"Use your eyes," said Markham. "The alarm was set."

"He's entitled to ask for the alarm information," said Sheena, "and insurers will need that information in writing from the alarm company in order to progress the claim."

Sheena, you are a star, I thought, not for the first time.

"If you send the letter to me by email today, I will contact the alarm company immediately so we can obtain a quick response, and I will copy Derek and Georgie in on the emails," I said.

"Fine," said Ronnie Stanshaw, "I will send you a letter by email today."

Warren looked slightly uneasy, Isaac wrinkled his nose and Markham glared, but none of them offered a reason as to why I could not contact the alarm company.

Chapter 2

Georgie and I commenced our inspection outside, making our own notes of the physical evidence and taking photographs. Isaac followed us and attempted to replicate our photographs.

The exteriors of the units in the industrial estate were well lit by lighting mounted on lamp posts, and I observed that none of the other industrial units had an external CCTV system. It was also clear from the inspection that no forced entries had been made to the Dagenham Glass building and that the warehouse access bay door had been unlocked and raised – for the fire brigade – as was described by Ronnie Stanshaw.

By this time, it was dusk, so we carried out a preliminary inspection inside the building by torchlight and I dictated my notes. The fork-lift truck was indeed parked next to but not connected to the charger in the access bay. The fork-lift truck, the charger and the access bay itself were only soot damaged. In particular, the fork-lift truck and charger had not suffered any direct fire damage that would have been expected if either had been the origin of the fire.

The initial inspection of the warehouse revealed no further physical evidence as to the origin or cause of the fire, but this was unsurprising. In cases such as this warehouse where there was a high fire load (cardboard boxes stored on pallets), which was well-ventilated (by virtue of the stock having been stored on open racking separated by aisles), the flaming fire would have spread quickly and would have been well-established throughout the warehouse before the fire brigade were able to deploy extinguishment water. In this regard, the fire would be expected to have caused severe damage to all the cardboard boxes and pallets, as was observed, so it was not necessary to invoke the involvement of a fire accelerant, such as petrol, to account for the pronounced damage, although such a possibility could not be discounted at this stage.

Various tests undertaken by the Fire Research Station in relation to other fires had shown that once established, the flames from a fire starting at the base of cardboard boxes stored on warehouse racking would spread upwards over the vertical surfaces of those boxes, reaching the top of typical racking in a minute or so. Other tests had shown that a single skin, corrugated, cement asbestos roof and plastic skylights fitted to such a roof – like the roof fitted to the Dagenham Glass building – could fail in less than a minute when exposed to a flaming fire. Given these test results and Mr Stanshaw's evidence that flames first emerged from the rear-left part of the roof, it seemed likely that the fire had started in that area of the warehouse but this was still a floor area of at least 5 metre x 5 metre, all of which was covered in fire debris to a depth of at least 1 metre.

"We'll need to excavate this," said Georgie, "but it's too dark to start now, so we should leave it until tomorrow."

Georgie never missed an opportunity to charge a client fees, I thought, although in fairness to her, in this case, the debris in the rear-left part of the warehouse did need to be removed, despite my scepticism that anything of significance would be found.

"You do know the fire brigade consider the fire was caused by an electrical fault?" asked Isaac.

"Did they check the light switches?" I asked.

Isaac's silence and wry smile spoke volumes.

"How do you know what the fire brigade think, anyway?" I asked, after letting the silence progress long enough for Isaac to feel uncomfortable, "They aren't here."

"The fire brigade were still here when I arrived on site this morning," said Isaac.

"You must have received instructions very quickly. The fire was only yesterday evening," I said.

"Harry called me late last night," said Isaac slowly.

"So, he learnt of the fire soon after it started then?" I said.

More silence from Isaac.

I was not surprised. There was a strong suspicion in the insurance industry that loss assessors received prompt information on very large fires from some members of the fire brigade who received cash payments in return. It was all too plausible that one of Markham's fire brigade informants had called him shortly after the fire brigade received the emergency call to the fire and that Markham had attended the scene to offer his services to Ronnie Stanshaw shortly after the fire brigade arrived.

"I can be here by half past eight tomorrow," I said, interrupting Isaac's silence.

"Yes," said Georgie, "I can be here at eight thirty."

"I should be here by then, but I don't want you to start until I arrive," said Isaac, attempting to regain control of the situation.

"Have you spoken to the woman from the double-glazing company, who discovered the fire?" I asked Isaac.

"I haven't had a chance yet," said Isaac defensively.

"We could speak to her now, before she leaves for the evening," I said.

Mary Wedge was a perfect witness from a fire investigator's perspective: friendly, enjoying the attention and open, seemingly to the point of naivety. The apparent innocence was a mask for a sharp intelligence and keen observational skills. Mary was the operations manager at the double-glazing firm occupying the unit opposite Dagenham Glass, and as was usual, after finishing work on the evening of the fire, she had gone outside to wait for her husband to collect her.

"I had been outside about five minutes, and had just finished reading a text from my husband who said he was going to be a few minutes late because he was stuck in traffic, when I noticed a small glow above the Dagenham Glass building. I had never seen that before, so I kept looking at it, and it quickly changed to flames," said Mary, blinking at me sweetly.

We were speaking to Mary outside the reception door of the double-glazing company, so I asked her, "So, from this position, could you direct us to where precisely you saw the flames?"

"There," said Mary, pointing to the top left of the Dagenham Glass front elevation. "But it was actually close to the rear of the roof, not the front," said Mary.

"How actually do you know that?" asked Isaac. "All we can see is the front of the Dagenham Glass building, which is high and prevents you seeing where something emerges from the roof."

"Before the fire, the apex of the roof was just visible and was parallel to the front of the building. The flames were emerging from behind the apex," said Mary, smiling brightly at Isaac.

"What did you do after seeing the flames?" asked Georgie.

"I called the fire brigade on my mobile," said Mary. "And after I called, I saw that Mr Stanshaw and his son, Warren, were getting into Warren's car, so I shouted to them that flames were coming from their roof. Mr Stanshaw came over to see me, but Warren just got into the car and drove off, which I thought was a bit odd," said Mary, pausing slightly for effect. "Anyway, I pointed out the flames to Mr Stanshaw," continued Mary, "and he immediately ran over to the Dagenham Glass building, unlocked the reception door, went in and switched the lights on. I became concerned so I ran over and saw him pick up a fire extinguisher in reception then go through an internal door. I was then even more concerned, so I went into the reception, opened the internal door and screamed along the corridor to him to come out. Thankfully, he did."

"What time did you call the fire brigade?" I asked.

"Twenty-two minutes past five; the time is recorded on my mobile," said Mary, showing us the relevant screen on her mobile telephone.

This information prompted a puzzled look from Georgie and heavy blinking accompanied by a blank stare from Isaac.

Mary subsequently confirmed that Warren drove back after a short time and that the fire brigade attended within ten minutes of the call by which time, flames were emerging from all of the roof. We thanked Mary for her assistance just as her husband arrived to collect her.

After she had departed, I said, "It is a little odd that Mrs Wedge called the fire brigade at 1722 hours. Michael said they had left the Dagenham Glass building just after five."

"He's obviously mistaken. Warren said they left some time after five," said Isaac, emphasising 'some time', "which is entirely consistent with what Mrs Wedge said."

"In which case, if Michael left the warehouse via the internal door at ten to five, they must have been talking in the upstairs office for almost half an hour before they left," said Georgie.

"Which is probably right. Time can pass quickly when you are chatting," said Isaac, slightly triumphantly, as he clearly thought he had won this argument.

I was uncomfortable with Isaac's explanation but decided not to pursue the discussion, partly because I did not want to reveal my line of reasoning, and also, I was distracted by the feeling that there was something I should have asked Mrs Wedge but had not. My silent pondering of the latter point resulted in a growing smile on Isaac's face, presumably because he thought I was trying to think of a counter-argument to his view on the timing.

"This is where experience counts," said Isaac. "I am going to report my findings to Harry and Mr Stanshaw. I will see you both tomorrow."

"What are you going to advise them caused the fire?" I asked.

"Isaac blinked rapidly for a few seconds, hesitated then said "That is confidential."

Not as keen on an electrical fault as earlier then, I thought.

After Isaac had departed to find Markham and Ronnie Stanshaw, Georgie said, "I will check my notes, but I am sure Michael said they had only been chatting a few minutes in the upstairs office and that he drove away just after five."

"He did," I said, "but Isaac is also right. Warren did say they left some time after five and time can pass quickly when you are talking to someone."

"So, that's what you think happened?" asked Georgie.

"I don't know, but until we receive the information from the alarm company, the time of call to the fire brigade is the only certain time we have," I replied.

"What was all that about whether Warren set the alarm? You

almost accused him of lying, and Markham was getting very wound up."

"No one smokes, and I cannot see how an electrical fault occurring inside steel conduit could initiate a fire amongst external stock, particularly as the lights were off. That only leaves arson, but there were no forced entries and flames were seen emerging from the roof shortly after they left. Knowing how rapidly fires spread upwards over the surfaces of cardboard boxes stored on racking and how quickly a cement asbestos roof fitted with skylights will fail when exposed to flames, it must be considered likely that the flaming fire started shortly before they left, so it is legitimate to wonder whether they deliberately started the fire. Given that all the warehouse aisles were protected by PIRs, I wondered whether Warren had left the alarm unset, gone into the warehouse, started the fire then left the building," I said.

"The key was in the set position, and Michael saw Warren set the alarm then come straight out," said Georgie.

"Apparently so," I said.

"You're not suggesting that it was a conspiracy involving Michael?" said Georgie.

"No, I don't like that. If the Stanshaws started it, they surely wouldn't have deliberately involved one of their van drivers in the plot," I said.

"I investigated a case once where a disgruntled employee started a fire just before they left their employer's premises," said Georgie.

"Yes, I've had one like that," I said, "but Michael didn't seem disgruntled, and his wife has just had their first child, so it seems unlikely he would risk his livelihood, unless he has another job lined up, which doesn't seem to be the case. Besides, the evidence of the Stanshaws and Michael is consistent that

Michael left the warehouse and went up to the office at ten to five, so if he had started the fire just before then, the flames would have been through the roof within a few minutes, after which the fire would have spread rapidly through the warehouse whilst they were still in the upstairs office, but it is in fact clear from Mrs Wedge's observations that the fire only started a short time before 1722 hours when she saw flames issuing from the roof."

"All of which seems to suggest that the fire wasn't deliberately started," said Georgie.

"Which is what Isaac will say," I said. "He will say that the only plausible explanation for the fire evidence is that the fire was caused by some form of electrical fault and that although the technical mechanism appears unlikely it is not impossible and simply illustrates the point that fires are rare events."

"I really don't like an electrical fault," said Georgie.

"As I've said, neither do I," I said. "And in relation to the warehouse lights, do you think there is any significance in Michael having been asked to start leaving a light on a month before the fire?"

"No. Anyway, he didn't yesterday evening."

"Even that is a little odd," I said, "that he forgot on the evening there was a fire."

"One of life's coincidences."

"Neither of us like coincidences, Georgie."

"I can't see how someone being asked to leave a light on then forgetting to do so has anything to do with the cause of the fire. If it was the other way round, I could see how there might be something in it but it's not. What are you going to advise your clients?"

"I'm going to say that accidental causes are unlikely but cannot be eliminated. I will also say that I have a concern that the fire was deliberately started by the insured but at this stage there is no positive evidence and we need to obtain the alarm information and excavate the debris."

"Whatever the arguments about what Michael saw when Warren Stanshaw reached into the cupboard containing the alarm control box, the alarm surely was set because it sounded when Mr Stanshaw walked back towards the building after Mrs Wedge alerted him to the fire. PIRs are designed to sense the moving infrared spectrum of an intruder, but we both know they can be activated by the infrared spectrum of burning stock falling in a fire, which is probably what happened."

"By the time Mr Stanshaw was walking back towards the building, the fire was clearly well developed as it had already broken through the roof and was probably spreading rapidly within the warehouse. PIRs will usually activate in response to the infrared spectrum produced by spreading flames before any stock has fallen so I am surprised that the alarm didn't activate prior to the fire breaking through the roof."

"The point is it did activate, so the alarm was set."

"If the alarm was not set, it would still have been activated when the fire affected the tamper wires, which are routed with the alarm signal wires around the walls between the PIRs and the alarm control box in reception. The fire would have taken a little while to spread to those wires, which might account for the apparent delay in the alarm sounding."

Georgie paused thoughtfully then said, "How do you account for the key being in the set position?"

"At the moment, I can't," I conceded, "but the alarm evidence should tell us whether it was set."

After a little further consideration, Georgie said, "Okay, I agree."

"So I think we should both be providing our clients with the same advice. I will send the email to the alarm company as soon as I receive Ronnie Stanshaw's authorisation email."

"Okay, see you tomorrow," said Georgie who then walked slowly to her car.

As she did so, Sheena walked out of the Dagenham Glass building with someone I recognised, Barry McGee, who worked for Carters, another firm of loss adjusters. Barry, noted for his cheerfulness, was good to work for as he liked to understand the detail of a case – and he had a healthy dislike for Harry Markham. He was frowning deeply as he approached with Sheena.

"Hello, James," said Barry, "I'm pleased you're on this one. I'm appointed by the building insurers, and Sheena and I agree that there are no issues between the building and contents insurers. We would like you and Georgie to work together on this one."

"That's fine, Barry, we already are."

"Pleased to hear it." said Barry, smiling. "I'll go and have a chat with Georgie."

After Barry left, I expressed my concerns to Sheena that an accidental cause was very unlikely and that the fire may have been deliberately started by the Stanshaws. I pointed out the odd points of evidence: that about a month before the fire, Michael was asked to leave a light on in the warehouse when he left but apparently forgot to do so on the evening of the fire; that Mrs Wedge had discovered the fire and called the fire brigade at 1722 hours, which was later than I had expected based on the evidence of the Stanshaws and Michael as to when they had apparently left the building; and that the intruder alarm, if set, seemed to have responded late to the developing fire. I also explained the counter arguments.

"So your concerns can be explained by Michael simply forgetting to switch off the light, something he had done previously; time passing quickly when people are chatting; and in the case of the alarm, the detectors simply responding late to a fire, an event they were not designed to detect," said Sheena slightly doubtfully. "Also, Michael has said that the Stanshaws did not go into the warehouse before leaving the building, which means there's no positive evidence the fire was deliberately started. On that basis, James, there's no case."

I had to accept Sheena had succinctly summarised the evidence as it would be viewed by insurers and any lawyer appointed by insurers.

"Sheena, at this stage, I can't advise insurers that I am content with the fire having been caused accidentally," I said, which ultimately was my best point for gaining time. "I will probably be in a better position to advise you on cause once I have the alarm evidence, which I might receive tomorrow. Also, provided you agree, I have arranged with Georgie and Isaac to start excavating the area where the fire probably started tomorrow morning, but the clearance might take a day or so."

"Insurers are going to come under huge pressure to accept liability on this, James. But actually, I am disturbed by what you have said, and Barry also doesn't like it. I will impress on insurers the importance of obtaining the alarm evidence, which will probably cause them to reserve their position for a short time. Go ahead with the excavation tomorrow, but can you call me as soon as you receive the alarm information?"

"Of course. Hopefully, that is tomorrow, but I will let you know if there is a problem."

"Thanks, James," said Sheena, and we departed with both of us deep in thought.

Whilst I was in the taxi on the way back to the office, Ronnie Stanshaw emailed a letter to me authorising the alarm company to provide me with information on the system installed at Dagenham Glass. I viewed the email on my mobile telephone, and during the journey, I emailed a letter to the alarm company asking for the specification for the alarm system and all the signals received from Dagenham Glass by the alarm company's central monitoring station, including set and unset times, for the past two weeks. I copied the email to Georgie and Isaac.

Chapter 3

I arrived at Jacobs' office at about half past six. The lights were blazing in many of the offices, as partners and associates who had also returned from inspections dealt with urgent matters on their various cases.

On my way to my first-floor office, I walked past Brian Dukes' office. Brian was an electrical engineer with an enthusiastic disposition. His office door was open, and seeing that he was not on the telephone, I stopped at his doorway.

"Hello, James, how are you?" asked Brian.

"I am fine, busy, busy. Where have you been today?"

"A domestic kitchen fire."

"Cause?"

"You tell me. A woman with one arm was frying sausages. She also developed amnesia after the fire."

"Oh, no! Not the 'I can't remember what happened' syndrome. They have always been involved in the cause one way or another. I suspect in your case, the oil in the pan caught fire and she got into difficulty because she only has one arm."

"Correct. She eventually had a memory recall whilst I was there. She had tried to extinguish the flames with a tea towel but that caught fire, so she threw it into the large plastic waste bin, and the fire really took off then."

"So, straightforward in the end?"

"The loss adjuster for the house insurers was disappointed because he instructed us on the case thinking the cause might be a fault with the hob and he could sue the manufacturers to recover the insurer's outlay."

"Don't complain. With loss adjusters like that, we will always be in business, Brian."

"What was your case?"

I briefly summarised the essential evidence of the Dagenham Glass fire.

"Phew, you've got a really interesting one there," said Brian.

"I'm back tomorrow to excavate the scene. Also, Markham and Isaac are involved, which doesn't help."

"Markham, Marty's mate," chuckled Brian.

"What?"

"Don't you know? Markham has joined Marty's golf club."

"I am astonished. Isn't Marty a member of the Imperial, Herts' best golf club?"

"Yes."

"So, how did Markham get in?"

"Apparently, he knows one of the members who is an insurance broker, which is what Markham was until three years ago."

"I wonder why he left insurance broking and became a fire-brigade-chasing loss assessor?"

"No idea but you can understand how his experience working for insurers would help him in the loss assessing world."

"I can... and he's friends with Marty?"

"No, but you can pull Marty's leg about it."

"I wonder if Markham dresses like a semi-house-trained gangster at the golf club?"

"Marty says not. He hardly recognised Markham when he first saw him there, which made for a bit of an awkward moment. Marty should be seeing him tonight actually. It's the golf club

AGM and Marty left at five to attend."

I didn't actually believe that Marty would become friends with Markham, but then I reflected that you never know someone as well as you think you do and that sometimes people have formed the most unlikely friendships. I surprised myself by making a mental note to be wary of providing Marty with too much information on my cases involving Markham.

In my office, I wrote a note for my secretary, Mavis, informing her that I was going straight to Dagenham Glass tomorrow. I then tried to settle down and complete an urgent letter report on one of my cases, a fire caused by a known fault involving a printed circuit board – a PCB – in a dishwasher, a report that I should have been able to finish quickly even after a tiring day at a scene. It was difficult, however, to stop my mind shifting to the Dagenham Glass case and the uneasy feeling that I had missed some important evidence, particularly with respect to what Mary Wedge had told me.

Eventually, necessity forced me back to the dishwasher fire report, and at about eight p.m., I emailed it to the client. I then shuffled the pile of other case files on my desk into a slightly different order of priority, which at least made me feel a little better with respect to workload.

Finally, I left the office and took the Underground to my home, a two-bedroom, first-floor flat in Archway, North London. My wife, Jemima, a lawyer in one of London's top law firms – we met on a case – was at a client's reception, and I was not expecting her home until about eleven p.m., so I picked up a Chinese takeaway on the walk from Archway tube station.

The flat overlooked a small park and was decorated in cool, pastel colours. The mainly traditional furniture had been purchased from high-street stores, but the kitchen was modern. The overall effect was very relaxing, and Jemima and I loved it as a haven from our demanding jobs. At least it was partly a retreat for me as I found it difficult to switch off from casework, as now, while I ate my meal and my muscles ached but my mind spun the options on the Dagenham Glass case.

I was still searching for solutions when I showered and afterwards when I sat on the sofa waiting for Jemima to return, with the other part of my brain fighting to make me sleep. Jemima broke the conflict when she returned, also tired, but with a ready smile and sparkling eyes.

"How is my preoccupied husband?" she said, throwing her arms around me as I stood up.

"Very happy now that I have got my gorgeous wife in my arms... my perceptive, gorgeous wife," I said, emphasising 'perceptive' and giving her a hug and a kiss.

"You were sitting on the sofa with no book, no newspaper and the television off," Jemima said, as explanation, kissing me.

I grinned. "Tell me about your day," I said.

"No, you first, then I'll tell you about mine; that way might help you switch off."

"You are too good," I replied, giving her another hug and kiss. I then summarised what had happened during the day while Jemima sat on the sofa listening attentively.

"Anything glare out at you?" I asked.

"I think Marty and Selena are having an affair," said Jemima.

"Reasoning?"

"Selena knew Marty was looking for an excuse not to do the Dagenham Glass case and was very keen to help him, which suggests a much closer relationship than would be expected between a partner and a secretary. Marty might also have left at five for a short assignation with Selena before going to the golf club AGM."

"I agree with your logic, but I was rather hoping you would apply your analytical mind to the Dagenham Glass case."

"Can't help you on the alarm or fire evidence, not my area of expertise. Only point I would make is that I am dealing with a fraud case at the moment and the critical evidence is the tachograph of the van that allegedly was used to drive away the stolen goods."

I metaphorically turned to stone. "My darling wife, you are a star," I eventually said, still statuesque.

"You've gone all stiff."

"Are we going to do anything about that?"

"You're not too tired then." she said, smiling.

"You've invigorated me in so many ways." I grinned back, pulling her up from the sofa and holding her close. "How was your day by the way?"

Later, we both slept soundly.

Chapter 4

The following morning, I took the Underground to Dagenham Heathway then a taxi to Dagenham Glass, arriving there at 0820 hours. Georgie and Isaac were already there, standing silently and thoughtfully a few metres apart.

"You look pleased with yourself," said Isaac.

I must, I thought because Isaac was not on my list of perceptive people.

"The thought of working with you all day is overwhelming," I replied as deadpan as I could manage.

Georgie glanced at me with raised eyebrows.

"Is Michael here?" I asked.

"You interviewed him yesterday," said Isaac.

"That sounds like 'Yes'… and there's his van," I said, looking to Isaac's left, "so he is here."

"He's collecting some things from the office to take to the temporary premises, so he will be leaving soon."

"I'll wait by his van then as it's really the van I'm interested in."

"The van, why do you want to see that?"

"The tachograph. Here's Michael now," I said, walking briskly over to the van, with Georgie and Isaac in hot pursuit.

"Good morning, Michael," I said as Michael approached pushing a trolley of cardboard boxes. "I appreciate you're busy, but before you go, could we view the van's tachograph readings for the day of the fire?"

"Yes, but I do need to be off soon," said Michael, opening the van doors.

"Hold on," said Isaac, blustering slightly, "you already know what time he left. Mary Wedge told us what time she called the fire brigade, and the van left just before then."

"All we know from Mary Wedge's evidence is the time she called the fire brigade. The tachograph will show the time the van left."

"You really shouldn't be wasting time on a minor point like this," said Isaac. "There is limited daylight today, and we should be using it to excavate the debris, as was agreed."

"Checking the tachograph will not take long and might actually settle the timing issue once and for all."

Isaac went into full blink mode as he no doubt contemplated the consequences of advising Michael not to show me the tachograph readings: suspicions would be heightened, and I would advise Sheena that the evidence was critical and that insurers should decline to accept the claim until the readings were obtained. I wondered also whether Isaac took into account that tachograph readings were incorruptible and would not be erased from the tachograph memory for a very long time.

"Okay," said Isaac, nodding to Michael, "let's do it. Then can we please get on with the excavation?"

Michael got into the van's cab, inserted his driver's card in the tachograph and pressed a few buttons. The display indicated that the van had been stationary all afternoon on the day of the fire and that at 1702 hours, the vehicle had commenced a five-mile journey, presumably to Michael's home, with that journey ending at 1718 hours.

"There's obviously about a twenty-minute error in the tachograph timing," said Isaac.

"We could check the accuracy of the timings by comparing the tachograph recordings with Michael's recollections as to when he started and ended journeys. For example, when did you arrive here today?" asked Georgie, looking at Michael.

"About quarter to eight," said Michael.

The tachograph recordings duly showed that earlier, the van had travelled five miles and had parked at 0746 hours. Further checking of the tachograph showed that in accordance with Michael's recollections, he had arrived at Dagenham Glass at 0745 hours on the day of the fire, had driven the van away – with stock for delivering – just after 0800 hours and had arrived back at the premises at 1310 hours, with all the timings being in accordance with his recollections.

"No sign of a timing error there," I said. And after receiving no response from Isaac, I continued, "Has anyone got any further questions for Michael?"

No one had any more questions, so we thanked Michael for his assistance.

"We need to check whether the time on Mary Wedge's mobile is accurate," said Isaac somewhat uncertainly after Michael had started loading the cardboard boxes into his van.

"I called the fire brigade yesterday evening, and they confirmed the time of the first call to the fire was Mary Wedge's at 1722 hours," said Georgie, frowning.

"There's obviously an error somewhere," said Isaac, uneasily.

"I think we should speak to Mrs Wedge," I said, observing that Mary Wedge had just been dropped off outside the double-glazing unit by her husband. I walked towards Mary, with Georgie and Isaac following.

"Good morning, Mary," I said, when Mrs Wedge turned as

I approached. "Sorry for disturbing you again, but could we ask you one question before you start work?"

"Of course, good morning," said Mary smiling.

"On the evening of the fire, just before Warren Stanshaw got in his car, did you see a van drive away from in front of the Dagenham Glass building?"

"No, there was no van."

"Hold on, Mrs Wedge," said Isaac with alarm in his voice, "you were looking at the flames coming from the roof and calling the fire brigade before you saw Warren Stanshaw get into his car, so you might have missed a van driving away."

"I don't think I did," said Mrs Wedge firmly.

"Did you see Mr Stanshaw and his son leave the Dagenham Glass building?" asked Georgie.

"I can't be certain that I did but I am sure that I did not see a van drive away."

No one had any further questions, so we thanked Mrs Wedge for her help and returned to the front of the Dagenham Glass building.

"She was clearly distracted," said Isaac. "She missed Ronnie and Warren – and Michael – coming out of the building, and she didn't see Michael driving the van away, a well-known witness fallibility."

"Of course, Mrs Wedge's recollections would be consistent with the tachograph time and the time of call to the fire brigade," I said quietly.

"Rubbish!" said Isaac slightly aggressively. "We know from Ronnie's and Warren's evidence that Michael drove the van away just before Mrs Wedge alerted them to the fire."

Neither Georgie nor I commented on this point.

"Should we start the excavation?" I asked after allowing a

couple of seconds of silence.

"I don't know what you have been suggesting," said Isaac, "but I think you need to be careful."

"I'm suggesting we start the excavation."

"You know what I mean."

"I think we should get a move on," I said, turning to my kit-bag to retrieve my overalls and boots.

Isaac decided not to pursue the timing issue, standing in disturbed silence whilst I got changed.

Georgie, who also appeared to be thinking deeply, continued moving the narrative away from the timing. "I have marked out a suggested excavation area on this plan," she said, holding up a drawing, which she had made during the previous day's inspection and which had the aisles in the rear-left corner of the building shaded in red.

"I'm content with that," I said.

Isaac gave an affirmative grunt.

The excavation proceeded far more quickly than I had anticipated as all three of us got to work, lifting and digging out the debris and moving it to one side. By mid-afternoon, the aisles in Georgie's shaded area had been cleared of debris down to the painted concrete floor. The paint was scorched in some places but was largely intact, having been protected from the fire by the collapsed debris. The paint was particularly scorched adjacent to the base of an approximately 2-metre-long section of racking in which the cardboard boxes exposed by the clearance of the debris had been destroyed down to the floor. By way of comparison, the lowest boxes in the adjacent racking had survived severe direct fire damage due to the protection provided by the collapsed debris.

What was clear to all three of us was that there was no pool-shaped scorching pattern on the painted floor, such as would have been expected if a flammable liquid, like petrol, had been burning there. Also, there were no remains of a petrol container on the floor and there were no smells of petrol residues amongst the debris at the base of the racking containing the destroyed boxes. I was sure that, like me, neither Georgie nor Isaac thought that a flammable liquid had been involved in the initiation of the fire.

"I am going to take a sample of debris for analysis," said Isaac, placing some of the charred debris from the racking containing the cardboard boxes that had been destroyed to floor level in a plastic sample bag. Georgie and I also collected samples, which we would all send for analysis by independent laboratories, with, in all likelihood, the results showing that no petrol residues were present.

Isaac continued, "This pattern of fire damage could easily be accounted for by an electrical fault at a high level causing hot debris to fall onto and ignite those cardboard boxes next to the floor. The fire would then have spread upward, and falling debris would have collapsed into the aisles and prevented the fire from damaging the other boxes next to the floor."

"Surely, if there was an electrical fault at a high level, the hot debris would be more likely to ignite cardboard boxes in the upper part of the racking," I said.

"If the electrical fault was above the aisles, then the hot debris could easily have fallen onto the boxes at the base of the racking," retorted Isaac.

"There is an alternative, simpler explanation for the severe damage to those cardboard boxes next to the floor in that racking," I said.

"There is no positive evidence that this fire was deliberately started," snapped Isaac.

"Interesting, you are the first person to mention the possibility of arson," I said, ignoring that Georgie and I had discussed the possibility yesterday.

"You've clearly been thinking that."

"You agree then that the pattern of damage could be readily accounted for by the direct application of a lit match or lighter to the cardboard boxes next to the floor."

"You know my views."

"It's nearly four o'clock," said Georgie. "We should check the electrical protection devices then call it a day."

The electrical circuit breakers were in a broom cupboard in the office block and were only soot damaged. Moreover, all of the circuit breakers protecting the warehouse circuits had tripped, which was unsurprising as we all knew that a circuit breaker trips when a fire burns the insulation from its circuit's wiring, and the exposed conductors, which are at different electrical potentials, touch, producing a large 'short circuit' overcurrent and a concomitant arc.

Isaac would no doubt argue that one of the circuit breakers protecting the warehouse lighting circuits had tripped first because of some form of electrical fault that caused the fire. In this regard, the transient high temperature arc caused by a short circuit fault overcurrent locally melts the wiring's copper conductors at the point of contact, and following some fires in which the temperature does not exceed about 1000° C (the melting point of copper), small beads of once-molten copper on the wiring indicate where a short circuit arc has occurred.

In the Dagenham Glass fire, however, all of the wiring that we recovered from the steel conduits in the area of excavation had either disintegrated or showed evidence of melting in many areas due to the temperature of the fire having exceeded the melting point of copper. As a result, any small beads of copper caused by arcing – either an effect or cause of the fire – were lost.

I suspected we all had reached the same conclusions concerning the electrical evidence, but given that it was not diagnostic in this case, no one was inclined to engage in a discussion of the minutiae.

"I don't think anything will be achieved by attending here tomorrow," I said.

"I agree," said Isaac.

"So do I," said Georgie. "Has the alarm company replied to your email?"

We all checked our mobile telephones and discovered that about half an hour earlier, the alarm company had indeed replied to my email, copying in Georgie and Isaac.

Chapter 5

The reply from the alarm company resulted in Isaac's blinking going into overdrive. The alarm company stated in the email that although their monitoring station had received an unset signal from the Dagenham Glass alarm system at 0730 hours on the day of the fire (when the first member of staff attended for work), the next signal received was a tamper alarm at 1724 hours: no set signal had been received. By way of comparison, unset and set signals had been received at appropriate times in the morning and evening on the workdays leading up to the fire.

"The fire must have caused a fault with the signalling," said Isaac.

"Really?" I said. "It didn't prevent the tamper signal from being sent. Also, the alarm company has said in the email that the system is a 'Redcare' and no fault was ever indicated."

A Redcare meant that every thirty seconds, the alarm company's central monitoring station sent a check signal to the Dagenham Glass alarm control box, which responded with a reply signal. If there had been a fault in either the alarm control box or on the signal line such that no reply was received, a fault would have been indicated at the monitoring station.

"It doesn't take the case anywhere," said Isaac. "It would have been more helpful if the set time had been recorded."

"The point is that no set time was recorded," I said.

"That's not a point," said Isaac.

"Perhaps the alarm wasn't set," I said.

"How do you account for the key being in the set position?" asked Isaac, bristling.

"Surely, all that shows is the key was in the set position. It doesn't show the alarm was set."

"Warren heard the 'set beeping noise' and saw the green 'set' light on the alarm control box, so we can be sure the alarm was set, and Warren wouldn't have left the building if the alarm hadn't been set. It's common sense."

"How do you account for the monitoring station not receiving a set signal?"

"I just said. There was a fault."

"I think we're in a circular argument."

"You need to decide if there is anything further that you want to do, but I've seen nothing to suggest the cause was anything other than accidental."

"We could ask for the alarm control box to be retained so that the memory chip can be interrogated at some stage, although I suspect it won't provide any additional information," said Georgie.

"Okay, if you can arrange that for us, Derek, I would be grateful," I said.

"All right," said Isaac, "but otherwise, I trust you will be advising your clients that there is no evidence the fire was deliberately started."

"We haven't said that, Derek," I said.

"What evidence is there the fire was deliberately started?"

"The only possible accidental cause is an electrical fault, and I've already told you why I think that is very unlikely. Whatever way you look at the timing – the tachograph or the call to the fire brigade – there is something wrong, and the alarm evidence is also a concern."

"None of that shows the fire was deliberately started, and you know it."

"Derek, I'm not advising my clients this fire was started accidentally."

"You're a fool."

"No, I'm not."

"You agree with me don't you, Georgie?" said Isaac.

"I can't recall saying that," said Georgie.

"I'll have you both if this case gets to court," said Isaac.

Neither Georgie nor I replied. Isaac chuckled and walked over to his car with a self-satisfied grin.

After he had left us, Georgie said, "I agree that the tachograph time and the time of Mrs Wedge's call to the fire brigade are inconsistent and also that it is odd that the alarm set time was not recorded by the monitoring station, but Isaac's right, isn't he. There is no positive evidence the fire was deliberately started, and Warren wouldn't have left the building without setting the alarm."

"What do you mean by positive evidence?"

"You know, no evidence a flammable liquid was involved."

"The evidence needs to be considered in its entirety. An accidental cause is very unlikely. Given also that the tachograph time and the fire brigade time of call are accurate, isn't the only explanation that Ronnie and Warren Stanshaw left with Michael just before 1702 hours, then Ronnie and Warren returned and subsequently left again just before 1722 hours."

Georgie stared at me silently for a long time. "How does that explain the alarm evidence?"

"If the alarm wasn't set, there would have been no set signal, which is what the alarm company has stated. As I have said previously, even with the alarm unset, a tamper signal would have been generated when the fire eventually burned through the alarm signal wires, which also would have produced a local audible alarm. The tamper signal received by the alarm monitoring station at 1724 hours was about the time that Ronnie Stanshaw heard the alarm sound."

"That doesn't explain why the alarm wasn't set, bearing in mind the key was in the set position. What about Warren driving off to alert Michael? He wouldn't have done that if Michael had left twenty minutes earlier? Also, we still haven't got a good explanation for Michael being asked to leave a light on in the warehouse a month before the fire but all the lights being off when the fire occurred."

"You agree though that the best explanation for the discrepancy between the tachograph time and the time of call to the fire brigade is that Ronnie and Warren Stanshaw returned to the building?"

"I need to think about it, James."

"Okay, so do I because I agree that the points you have just raised need explaining. Let's think about it this evening and speak tomorrow before we advise our respective clients."

"Fine, I'll call you at ten tomorrow."

We then exchanged goodbyes and went our separate ways. I decided to go back to the office, arriving there at half past five.

As I entered Jacobs' offices, Jane Gainor, a metallurgist associate, who had been with Jacobs for four years, was leaving. Jane was beautiful, had a ready smile, was very self-contained and had a quiet, confident intelligence. I knew she had travelled to Truro earlier in the week to give evidence in her first case to go to trial, an incident in which the failure of a plumbing system fitting had resulted in a large water escape. Unfortunately, the owners of the property, a large manor house, were on holiday when the leak occurred so the property had suffered severe water damage.

"Hello, Jane, how did the court case go?" I asked.

"I think it went well," replied Jane. "The judge seemed to like my evidence that the fitting had been incorrectly installed, and she didn't like the plumber's expert's evidence that the fitting had been poorly manufactured. The judge said she would hand down judgement next week, so fingers crossed until then."

"Who was the plumber's expert?"

"A local guy, a semi-retired plumber who liked to hear himself speak but fell apart under cross-examination. He knew nothing about metallurgy. Harry Markham was also there and got into a bit of trouble with the judge for over-egging the insured's claim."

"Really, when was Markham there?"

"Tuesday."

"Tuesday, that's odd; I saw him at a scene in East London on Wednesday."

"What's odd about that? He left Truro on Tuesday evening. He nearly got into trouble with the judge on that as well. Markham's barrister asked the judge if Markham could give his evidence first on Tuesday morning as he had an engagement in Hertfordshire in the evening. When the judge enquired what the engagement was, the barrister said it was Markham's golf club AGM, which didn't impress the judge who wanted the witnesses to give evidence in a specific order. He told Markham he had to give evidence in the afternoon. Are you all right, James?"

Jane had clearly seen my jaw falling open as she was speaking.

"Yes," I said unconvincingly, "only the scene I was at yesterday and today was a fire that occurred shortly after 1700 hours on Tuesday evening. It would have been difficult for Markham to have attended there and offered his services to the insured if he didn't leave Truro until sometime on Tuesday afternoon, particularly if he was going to a golf club AGM. What time did he leave Truro on Tuesday?"

"He finished his evidence at four when the court adjourned. When I left the courtroom shortly afterwards, he was in the lobby making a phone call. He then ran out to a taxi, presumably to take him to the railway station."

"Very interesting, Jane. I've already got enough to think about on my case, and now I've got something else. Anyway, your case sounds like it went well. I look forward to hearing the result."

"Thanks," said Jane and left smiling.

Chapter 6

I climbed the stairs slowly to my office, contemplating how Markham could have been in two places at once on Tuesday evening, both of which were evidently remote from Truro. In my office, I checked the train times on the National Rail app on my mobile. The earliest train that Markham could have caught from Truro on Tuesday evening was the 1655 hours, which had arrived at London Paddington at 2129 hours. It would have taken him a good hour to travel from there to Dagenham Glass.

I lifted my office telephone and dialled Marty's office number. He answered, so no Selena this evening.

"James, how are you?" he asked.

"I am fine, thanks. Marty, could I ask you about Harry Markham?"

"Sure," Marty said smoothly, "come on up."

When I entered Marty's office, he was looking at a case instruction sheet, which was used for writing down details when a client rang in with a new case. I initially thought he was going to ask me if I could take on the new case, but to my surprise, he said, "I am doing this one tomorrow, a mobile home fire near Maidstone, and Markham is actually involved in it."

"Maidstone, so when was that fire?"

"About four o'clock today; why?"

"Markham was at the Dagenham Glass scene with me all day yesterday, so I wondered how he could have offered his services on your mobile home fire, if for example, the mobile home fire had been yesterday. I'm still wondering actually. It's only quarter to six now and his office is in North London, so he must have moved very quickly to travel down to Maidstone this afternoon and offer his services to the insured on this one, even if one of his fire brigade contacts called him shortly after the fire brigade received the call."

"Barry McGee, the loss adjuster who has just called in the instructions on the mobile home fire, was in Kent on another case today, and he said that Markham was already at the scene when he arrived at five o'clock. Apparently, Markham had also been in Kent on a different case and had dropped into the mobile home fire on his way home."

"Markham's movements fill me with wonder."

"Why?"

"Jane has just told me that Markham was in court in Truro on Tuesday and that his barrister asked the judge if he could give evidence early because he was attending a golf club AGM in Hertfordshire that evening. As I understand it, Markham attended the AGM at your golf club in Hertfordshire yesterday evening; that's Wednesday evening, not Tuesday evening."

"He did attend my golf club AGM on Wednesday evening," said Marty slowly.

"Presumably, he's not a member of another golf club in Hertfordshire, which had its AGM on Tuesday?"

"I doubt it, given our annual membership fees," said Marty, smiling. "And I've never heard of anyone being a member of two golf clubs, but I can make enquiries about Marty if you like."

"Okay, thanks. The other problem with Tuesday evening is that the Dagenham Glass fire started sometime after 1700 hours and Markham couldn't have got back to London until 2129 hours, which means he couldn't have arrived at Dagenham Glass until 2230 hours at the earliest, assuming also that one of his contacts in the fire brigade called him about the fire whilst he was on the train from Truro. It seems incredible that Markham managed to sell his services to the Dagenham Glass owner on that job. Surely, there were other loss assessors who attended the scene before Markham. He was even taking a risk attending at 2230 hours. The insured might have left the scene before then."

"James, Markham is a loss assessor, and he rides his luck. He was in Maidstone at the right time today to pick up the mobile home fire, like Barry McGee, the loss adjuster for the insurers. Markham probably did take a flyer and turn up at the Dagenham Glass scene at half past ten on Tuesday night and found the insured still there, with no other loss assessors there because their fire brigade contacts weren't as good as his. That's how he gets cases and he's got to move quickly. Loss assessing is a cut-throat business."

"If that's right, I wonder what he was really intending to do on Tuesday evening, something he didn't want to tell the judge in Truro."

"Might be something in his private life."

Like an affair, I thought but decided not to say that to Marty.

"By the way," Marty continued, "Markham hunted me down at the AGM to claim that you had quote 'made a fool of yourself' at the Dagenham Glass case. I asked him how, and he said that you were implying that the alarm had not been set but that when you checked the alarm control box, the key was in the set position and the soot patterns showed it was in the set position at the time of the fire. I pointed out to him that that only showed the key was in the set position, it did not show the alarm was set, which he didn't like."

"Thanks, and well done. Today, Dagenham Glass' alarm

company said that they never received a set signal on Tuesday evening and that it was a Redcare system, with no indication of a fault either at the alarm control box or on the signal line. Mind you, I still haven't explained why the alarm didn't set."

"If a door fitted with alarm contacts was left open, the alarm wouldn't have set when the key was turned to the set position but a fault signal for the relevant alarm circuit would have been indicated at the alarm control box, so whoever had tried to set the alarm would have known that it hadn't set and would have looked for the cause of the fault."

"That was the owner's son, and the owner and van driver who were waiting outside for him both said that he came straight outside after reaching into the alarm control box cupboard."

"He wouldn't have left if a fault signal was indicated because he'd have known the alarm hadn't set."

"He said he didn't receive a fault signal. Hold on, he would have left if he had started the fire! That's it! If he had started the fire, then the PIR in that part of the warehouse could have sensed the fire like it senses an intruder, producing a fault signal when an attempt was made to set the alarm – in the same way that leaving a door with alarm contacts open produces a fault signal and prevents the alarm from being set.

"After starting the fire in the warehouse, he would have made his way to the reception area and turned the key in the alarm control box to the set position, but he is lying when he said he saw a green set light and heard the set beeping noise. The alarm control box almost certainly indicated a red fault light for the PIR in the part of the warehouse where the fire had started and prevented the alarm from setting, but he walked out leaving the key in the set position without attempting to rectify the fault because he knew he couldn't as one way or another the fault was being caused by the fire that he had started.

"In fact, he has lied twice because he initially left with his father and the van driver just after five when, I am now sure, he only pretended to set the alarm. He then returned with his father, started the fire and failed to set the alarm as I have just described. He didn't set the alarm on the first occasion they left because he knew that the subsequent unset signal would show that someone had returned."

"Do you think that they initially left with the van driver so that he could unwittingly provide them with an alibi?"

"I do and they were very keen for me to interview the van driver who almost did provide an alibi by saying that he saw the alarm being set, that no one went back into the warehouse after ten to five and that he left the building with the owner and son, but it backfired because they forgot that the van has a tachograph and they didn't know that the fire, which they subsequently started, would be through the roof in a couple of minutes – or that a witness outside the opposite unit would see the flames and alert them shortly after they left."

"Unlucky." Marty grinned.

"Let me know how you get on with the mobile home – and what Markham has to say for himself," I said as I turned towards the door.

"Don't worry about him; he's harmless, James."

"I am not convinced," I said as I left Marty's office.

I returned to my office, and with adrenalin fighting tiredness, I pondered many puzzles, mainly involving Dagenham Glass and Markham. I almost immediately mentally kicked myself because I had broken my vow not to provide Marty with too many details of my cases involving Markham, but I partly excused myself as I had wanted to check with him the day of his golf club AGM.

Also, in fairness to Marty, he had informed me what Markham was saying about me and had defended my logic when Markham had tried to ridicule me. Perhaps, more importantly, his comments on the door contacts, I was sure, had helped me solve the alarm evidence. Was it just paranoia that made me wonder what Marty would say to Markham tomorrow?

I reshuffled my files and made my way home. I took the Dagenham Glass file with me in order to read all my notes on the tube. I wanted to work out what I was going to say to Sheena and Georgie tomorrow and in what order.

After reading the notes, I slipped them slowly into my briefcase. I was reasonably sure I could explain the various queries relating to the fire, and I had an inkling as to an explanation for Markham's actions.

"My, you have had a good day," said Jemima when I entered the flat.

"I am close to solving the Dagenham Glass case," I said, slipping my arm around her waist, pulling her close and looking into her eyes. "And your tachograph idea was key, so thank you. How was your day? You look tired."

"Yes, I have just been in ten minutes. I spent the entire day preparing bundles of documents for a court case, but I got it done!"

"Excellent! Since we're both tired, let's just go out for dinner. It's Thursday so we should just be able to walk into a pub or restaurant."

And that is what we did. We went to a pub near Archway station and had a bar meal. After we had eaten, we mainly sat in companionable silence with occasional, easy chitchat, then Jemima said, "So, tell me what happened today."

I summarised the essential details and raised my eyebrows for comments.

"I think Marty is on your side, or at least he's on Jacobs' side. He immediately put a stop to Markham trying to criticise you, and he helped you solve the alarm evidence. He is probably wary of you because the shenanigans, when you went into his office with the Dagenham Glass instructions the other day, must have made him near certain you know of his relationship with Selena."

"I wonder if that is why he told me he was doing the mobile home case in Maidstone tomorrow – to earn some brownie points? He wouldn't normally do that sort of case."

"Doesn't Selena live near Maidstone?"

I hesitated. "She does," I said slowly, "but I'd be surprised if they had managed to arrange anything. The case came in after Selena would have left, so she couldn't have asked for a day off in order to meet up with Marty after he's done the case tomorrow."

"Just a thought." Jemima then moved on to Dagenham Glass. "Do you think Warren Stanshaw is someone who is likely to panic?"

"Yes," I replied immediately, "and I have already thought that explains a few issues."

We walked home and went to bed in companionable nakedness.

Chapter 7

The next morning, Friday, I arrived at the office at seven thirty and started drafting a preliminary report for Sheena, with the intention being also that my thoughts would be crystallised before I called her at nine o'clock. I did not want to leave speaking with Sheena until after I had spoken to Georgie at ten o'clock because notwithstanding that it would be helpful to know Georgie's views, I wanted to know, firstly, if Sheena was on board with my conclusions, and also I didn't want her to be ambushed by Barry McGee if Georgie called him early with her conclusions.

At eight thirty, the main office telephone rang, as was indicated by an illuminated button on the individual office telephones. It was Jacobs' policy to answer incoming calls within three rings, and as I knew Selena wouldn't be in until nine o'clock, I picked up my telephone and pressed the illuminated button.

It was Selena. "Oh, hello, James," she said weakly, "unfortunately, I have a tummy upset so I won't be in today."

I resisted the temptation to say, "Enjoy your day," and simply said, "Sorry to hear that. Get well soon, see you..." I then hesitated, stopped myself saying 'tomorrow' and said "some time."

"Thank you, bye," said Selena, even more weakly.

"Bye."

So Marty had taken the mobile home case because he saw

an opportunity, and he must have called or texted Selena yesterday evening. I suspected he would attend the mobile home scene this morning and spend the rest of the day out on manoeuvres with Selena.

I called Sheena and explained my views on the Dagenham Glass case.

"How confident are you about the alarm evidence explanation?" asked Sheena.

"Very confident, but if the case goes to court, I would need to do a test to demonstrate that these particular PIR sensors, which are specified in the information provided by the alarm company, do respond to a developing fire in their field of view. Also, we would need to interrogate the alarm control box."

"The Stanshaws returning to the building is certainly a compelling explanation for the alarm evidence and for the discrepancy between the tachograph time and the time of call to the fire brigade, but even in those circumstances, the deliberate conclusion relies also on there being no plausible accidental cause."

"Which is the case whatever the explanation for the alarm evidence or timing, although I think also that if a court of law concluded the Stanshaws had returned, the court would be unlikely to be sympathetic to an accidental cause."

"What about the samples you retained?"

"I'll arrange for them to be tested, but I am sure there will be no petrol residues. I think it is most likely that a naked flame was applied to the cardboard boxes at the base of a rack."

"If you're right on the timing, why did Warren drive off to alert Michael? He would have known that Michael had left twenty minutes earlier so he had no hope of catching him."

"I don't think he did drive off to alert Michael. I think that when Mary Wedge alerted Warren and his father to the fire – which they had started and which they hadn't expected to be breaching the roof when they departed – Warren pressed the panic button and simply drove off to leave the scene of the crime."

"Leaving his father there?"

"His father can't have been impressed."

"What about Michael being asked to start leaving a warehouse light on a month before the fire but all the lights being off when the fire occurred?"

"I think this fire had been planned for some time and that Michael was asked to start leaving a light on so that on the evening of the fire there would be an obvious accidental cause involving hot debris falling from an alleged fault involving the energised fluorescent light. Isaac has been trying to say there was a spontaneous electrical fault on the electrical wiring in the steel conduit, but it is not really plausible, and there are no other accidental causes in the warehouse.

"I think Michael did leave a light on when he left the warehouse at ten to five and that the Stanshaws switched on some more lights when they returned and went into the warehouse to start the fire. Given that Ronnie Stanshaw was haranguing Warren when we entered the meeting room the other day after observing all the light switches were off, I suspect that Warren was last to leave the warehouse and because he was in a bit of a panic, he switched off all the lights.

"On a similar point, I don't know who attempted to set the alarm finally. Ronnie and Warren Stanshaw were probably both at the alarm control box together and they realised that they had to leave the key in the set position even though the alarm hadn't set. That experience probably heightened Warren's panic so he was probably extremely jittery when Mary Wedge alerted them to the fire."

Sheena was silent for a few seconds then said, "I think insurers will want to put this evidence before a barrister to decide whether or not to decline the claim, and the pressure on them from Markham to accept the claim is already immense. I would like a preliminary report ASAP: today if possible, Monday at the latest."

"No problem, Sheena," I replied, mentally gulping. "I will also speak to Georgie and check if she is in agreement with me. If there is any issue, I will let you know."

"Thanks, James. I look forward to receiving the prelim."

I put the telephone down, but it rang almost immediately. It was Georgie, who skipped 'good morning'. "I think the alarm was prevented from setting because the fire was being sensed by one of the PIRs," she said.

"I agree, Georgie," I replied, then described my explanations for the other evidence.

"I think you're probably right, James, but I'm not sure it's enough to show the fire was deliberately started by the Stanshaws."

"Ultimately, that will probably be a matter for a court to decide and in the first instance for a barrister to provide a legal opinion as to whether my principals, the contents and business interruption insurers, settle the claim."

"My principals, the building insurers, will simply pay up as their insured, the building owners, weren't involved. Also, there can be no claim against them by the Stanshaws."

"What will you advise your insurers?"

"I will say that Ronnie and Warren Stanshaw returned to the warehouse and that the fire likely resulted from their actions."

Which is a cop out, I thought but decided not to ask her what action she had in mind.

"Okay, thanks, Georgie."

"Thanks, James. Good to work with you."

I hesitated as I was not used to an implied compliment from our rival firm. "Likewise, Georgie," I replied – and just about meant it.

As soon as we finished the call, I put considerations of my other cases to one side and started dictating a preliminary report for Sheena, determined to finish it by the end of the day, whatever else occurred. I had made the latter vow on previous cases and had been overrun by subsequent events but I had to set the target.

After half an hour, Simon, the associate whom I was supervising, came into the office and asked me to check a report that needed to be issued on Monday at the latest to meet our code of service. Simon was a bespectacled, intense physicist with close-cropped, fair hair who had been with us a year. He was very good technically but was rightly aware that he still had a lot to learn, which sometimes resulted in him being less certain with his conclusions than he should be.

Simon said that his report concerned a fire in a commercial kitchen extraction ductwork which had been positioned too close to timber structures, and the report involved a consideration of compliance with various building regulations. It was a full report that might not be straightforward to check. I told Simon that I would check the report today, but it might not be until later in the afternoon as I needed to keep my mind focused on my preliminary report. Simon knew that meant he might have to revise his report over the weekend in order to issue it on Monday morning, but he accepted that with good grace.

I continued with my preliminary report, but at about half past eleven, a new case came in involving a dishwasher in a West End restaurant, and the loss adjuster wanted an immediate attendance. Simon said he would go, and that left me as the only remaining fire investigator in the office as all the others were again out.

Thankfully, my luck held, and I finished dictating the preliminary report. I then gave the Dictaphone memory chip to Mavis for formalising into a Jacobs' report using proprietary software and went out to buy a sandwich.

I returned to the office and started checking Simon's report whilst eating a very late lunch. Simon's report was actually well written, and I had made good headway with it, making only a few suggested amendments to the text when Mavis, who was also Simon's secretary, came in and informed me that my preliminary report was ready for checking.

Mavis was tall, slim, dark-haired, married and a very efficient, calm, discreet secretary with a pleasant personality. For different reasons, I felt as lucky to have Mavis as a secretary as I did to have Jemima as a wife.

"Thank you, Mavis," I said. "I'll check my report shortly. I'm also checking Simon's report, and I don't think there are too many issues, but both reports will need to go out on Monday at the latest."

"No problem, James. Simon has just called in, actually. He should be finished and back within an hour."

I looked at my watch. It was three o'clock. "Excellent, it is all going too well!"

Mavis smiled. My mobile phone then rang and Mavis laughed as she left my office.

It was Barry McGee. "Thank you for your assistance on Dagenham Glass, James. Georgie's told me your views. I think you're right. Georgie's been a bit more circumspect but it's not a problem as there are no issues for my client. James, I've got a new case, and I'd like you to deal with it."

"Fine, what are the details?"

"It's a fire in a large, detached dwelling-house at the end of a secluded lane on the outskirts of Maidstone."

"Really, you know Marty has been doing your mobile home fire there today?"

"Yes, and Markham has been there as well, but there was no need for me to be there so I've been in the office all day dealing with Dagenham Glass and this case. Insurers just gave me the go-ahead to appoint you on this case five minutes ago, and I called Marty out of courtesy, but I only got his voicemail. I left a message about this case, but it doesn't matter though. He couldn't really have done much today as it will be dark soon and, as I will describe shortly, there are some reports that need to be considered before anyone thinks about attending the scene. Also, James, as I said, I'd like you to do it."

"No problem, Barry, I can do it. I only mentioned Marty in case you needed an urgent attendance today."

"No, the fire was actually eight months ago, in March, and it is a difficult case, James. The fire was investigated by Georgie shortly after the incident as the insurers of the property like Willoughbys, but those insurers have now asked for someone to review the evidence and look again at the scene. I have recommended you. I can send you Georgie's report, but in essence, the insured, a Mr Gerash, owns a property development company with a business partner and bought the risk property privately as his own residence about a year before the fire.

"I have some doubts as to whether Mr Gerash ever occupied the property. He said he had been living there but that a few weeks prior to the fire, he had removed most of the contents so that the property could be decorated and he was living with his girlfriend in her flat in Margate.

"The fire started in the ground-floor hall and spread up the stairs into the roof, which was severely damaged, and the remains of the roof collapsed through the ceilings into the first-floor rooms, resulting in extensive damage to those rooms."

"What was the cause?"

"The fire brigade and Georgie agree that the fire started amongst some plastic bags containing waste wallpaper and other waste decorating materials that had been left in the hall for disposal. There was also a portable, radiant halogen heater in the hall, and they think that it could have ignited the bags."

"Why was the heater plugged in and switched on?"

"The contract decorators who were working in the property on the day of the fire said that the heater wasn't plugged in when they left at five in the afternoon. As usual, Mr Gerash arrived before the decorators departed in order to lock up, and he said that after the decorators left, he decided to switch on the heater to warm up the property whilst he had a look around to check how the decorating was progressing. He said that he was also pre-occupied thinking about his business and that he simply forgot to switch off the heater when he left at about half five."

"It's just about plausible he would have switched on the heater for the short time he was in there and that he forgot to switch it off when he left, but the heater would have had a safety grille over the radiant elements, so I'm surprised it set fire to bags of waste unless they were very close to it – and if they were that close, it would have been foolish to have switched on the heater."

"Georgie essentially said the same thing as she did some tests which showed that the heater would only ignite bags of waste if they were positioned against or very close to the safety grille. We told the insured this, and he said that when he switched the heater on, the bags weren't directly in front of it but were in a pile to one side. He said that he had slammed the front door when he left, and he surmised that this might have caused some of the bags to collapse onto the front of the heater."

"I don't like it but I couldn't say it's not possible, and in fairness to the insured, he isn't a fire expert and he doesn't have to identify the cause, as we both know. We have to show what the cause is, and in particular, if we think the fire was deliberately started by the insured, we would have to find very compelling evidence, which I don't think is there on what you've said."

"That's what Georgie said."

"What time was the fire?"

"The occupier of the only other property in the lane, about 100 metres away, looked out of his kitchen window and saw a flickering glow in the area of the risk property at about eight p.m., about two and a half hours after Mr Gerash had left. This neighbour went outside, saw flames and called the fire brigade. The time of call was 2005 hours."

"So, if the bags of waste had fallen against the heater – which was left switched on – the bags could have melted and a smoulder could have been initiated in the waste paper. That smoulder, in turn, could have developed to a flaming fire within one to two hours. The fire could then have been through the roof by eight o'clock."

"Again, that is what Georgie said."

"What about smokers?"

"Neither the insured nor the decorators were smokers, and no one else visited the property during the day."

"Someone could have gone into the property at some time between the insured leaving and eight o'clock, and deliberately started the fire."

"That someone would have to have had access to keys because the fire brigade said that even though the fire was breaching the roof when they arrived, all the doors and windows were secure. On that point, the insured said that the loft hatch at the top of the stairs was open because he intended taking some timbers into the roof space to install a timber storage platform after the decorators had finished. It looks like the fire went straight up the stairs and into the roof."

"So when the burning remains of the roof collapsed into the first-floor rooms, the fire vented up through the destroyed ceilings. The fire didn't vent laterally through the windows, which is why the fire brigade found them secure."

"That's what Georgie said."

"Of course, the loft hatch might have been deliberately left open in the belief that this would assist with fire spread up the stairs, which it did to a certain extent. It's also a worry that the decorating might have been contrived to provide an excuse to move the contents out before the fire occurred."

"Yes."

"But there's no physical evidence to show the insured's explanations are false?"

"No."

"So I can read Georgie's report and visit the scene, but unless I notice some fantastic evidence that everyone's missed, I think I'll probably be agreeing with her. How much of the scene is still available?"

"Almost all of it, but Georgie has the heater, and the few burnt remains of the bags of waste have been cleared. Also, there are a few other matters you need to be aware of."

"Go on."

"Insurers were obviously concerned that the fire could have been deliberately started, and they stalled accepting liability whilst their special investigators carried out further enquiries. Those investigators quickly discovered that Mr Gerash was in dispute with his business partner concerning the dividends to be paid out by their property development business. That business partner subsequently alleged that Mr Gerash wanted to redevelop the incident property but couldn't afford to so deliberately started the fire to obtain the insurance money. Unfortunately, the business partner refused to sign a statement and has recently retracted the allegations, possibly because there has been a reconciliation with Mr Gerash."

"That can't have made insurers feel any easier."

"No, and it gets worse. Markham has been involved from the beginning, and one of the reasons that insurers stalled accepting liability is that they had never been presented with a formal claim. Two weeks ago, Markham submitted a formal claim on behalf of Mr Gerash, and the contents claim included a large number of expensive Boss suits, Armani shirts and other items of clothing, as well as about two hundred pairs of expensive shoes and training shoes."

"Didn't you say that most of the contents had been removed?"

"I did but Mr Gerash has said that all of this clothing and shoes had been left in the property in a pile on the bed in the main bedroom and covered with a dust sheet as protection from the decorating, and Georgie's photographs do show a burnt pile of what looks like clothing and shoes on the bed. Unfortunately, she never examined that pile when she carried out her inspection of the property."

"I'm not convinced that I would have examined it. It was

remote from the origin of the fire so was unlikely to provide any evidence on causation and was probably partly buried under collapsed roofing timbers. Also, Georgie couldn't have anticipated what seems to have been a subsequent exaggerated contents claim."

"The problem is that about a month ago, Markham appointed Isaac to investigate the cause. He went through those items on the bed, and he found some shoes, training shoes and some clothing items with Armani and Boss labels, far less than the number claimed, but Markham simply says the fire destroyed the remaining items."

"Why did Isaac inspect the items on the bed, given that they couldn't assist with causation?"

"He was asked to by Markham to assist with the contents claim."

"Have you got his report?"

"Yes, I can send it with Georgie's report."

Has Georgie now examined the clothing, training shoes and shoes?"

"No, she has asked to, but I have asked her to hold off for the time being."

"Does Georgie know that you are instructing me?"

"I told her a week ago that insurers would probably be asking another company to review the evidence and that I would be recommending you. She said she was comfortable with that."

"Are the items of clothing and shoes still at the property?"

"Yes, and I have asked Markham to tell the insured not to move them."

"Clearly, someone, either Georgie or I, should examine the clothing and shoes, and if I was to examine them, I could use that as an excuse to look at the property as well."

"Fine, I will speak to Markham about access and come back to you."

"Out of courtesy, we should tell Georgie that I will be attending the scene to look in particular at those items."

"I will speak to her."

"Thanks, Barry." We then exchanged goodbyes, and the conversation ended.

I continued checking Simon's report and had just completed it when Simon himself walked in.

"Simon, I've just finished your report. It reads well. I've only made a few suggested amendments, which I've highlighted. If you're happy to make those, it can go."

"Great, thanks. I'll look at it now."

"How was today's case?"

"It was fine. The fire started at the PCB in the control panel of the dishwasher, and the restaurant was mainly smoke damaged. Harry Markham arrived whilst I was there and persuaded the insured to accept his services... very smoothly done."

"I thought Markham was at a case in Maidstone with Marty today."

"Markham arrived at the restaurant at two o'clock. He told me that he had been with Marty in Maidstone in the morning and that they had finished at twelve thirty."

I smiled wryly and unkindly wondered whether Marty would squirm over his afternoon activities, assuming I was right that he had met Selena. Marty wouldn't know that Markham had told Simon they had finished in Maidstone at twelve thirty. He would, however, eventually find Barry McGee's three o'clock voicemail message so he would expect Barry to have rung into Jacobs' office with instructions on the property fire in Maidstone. It followed that he would need an explanation ready as to why he wasn't available on his mobile for Barry. Marty might simply say he decided to drive straight home and that his mobile must have lost its signal, but given that driving from Maidstone to Hertfordshire would only take about two hours, timing was critical, and I suspected he would pre-empt any potential query.

"What did Markham have to say for himself?" I asked Simon.

"That's the other reason I came to see you, actually. I had never met him before, and he looked uncomfortable when he saw me in Jacobs' overalls. He said he hoped I wasn't going to cause problems like you do. He also said Marty wasn't much better today."

"What did you say?"

"I said neither you, Marty nor I ever intentionally cause problems."

"Good answer."

"He also said he is dealing with one other case in Maidstone and that the loss adjuster was talking about getting Jacobs' to review the case. He wanted to know whether I had heard about it and whether anyone was doing it."

"The loss adjuster rang in on that case this afternoon, and I'll be doing it, which will probably ruin Markham's day. Did Markham actually say he was dealing with 'one other case in Maidstone' or 'another case in Maidstone'?"

"'One other case.' He said he's only done the case with Marty and the one that you're going to review, in Kent this year. He was moaning about the traffic. He said that every time he has been down to Maidstone on those two cases, he has got stuck in a jam. Is there an issue on the number of cases he has done in Maidstone?"

"I am interested in how Markham seems to pop up very quickly on some cases."

"I certainly think he has a contact in the London Fire Brigade and that contact spoke to him about my West End restaurant fire either whilst he was at Marty's scene or as he drove back from that scene."

"I'm sure that's right."

Simon then departed to finalise his report, and I checked my preliminary report on Dagenham Glass. As usual, Mavis had formalised it flawlessly, and after making a few nuanced changes on emphasis, I emailed it to Sheena.

Publish and be damned, I thought, because unlike Georgie, I certainly had said that the most likely explanation for the fire was that Ronnie and Warren Stanshaw had returned to the Dagenham Glass building and deliberately started the fire.

Chapter 8

The time was then almost five o'clock and the telephone rang. It was Marty.

"James, my apologies, I forgot to charge my mobile phone last night and it died whilst I was at today's scene. I drove home and put it on charge, but five minutes ago I noticed there was a voicemail from Barry McGee with a new instruction for Maidstone, although he did say it wasn't one for doing today. It looks as though he called at three o'clock whilst I was in the loo, and I didn't hear the call. Did he call into the office with the case?"

I thought it was a reasonably watertight story from Marty's perspective because his wife worked in the city so wouldn't be home yet and, crucially, wouldn't know when he had arrived home if the question arose. I strongly suspected he had just arrived home after his afternoon engaged in Ugandan discussions with Selena but I didn't want to pursue that.

"He did," I replied to Marty's question, "but although it is a serious case, it isn't one that needed doing this afternoon. It involves reviewing some reports prepared by Georgie and Isaac first before inspecting the scene, and Barry's asked me to deal with it. He was just calling you out of courtesy."

"Interesting. When I was at the mobile home scene, Markham did mention one other case he was dealing with in Maidstone that he was sure we were going to be asked to review and he wondered if I had heard anything about it. I said I hadn't but it was possible we had been instructed and that someone else was dealing with it. When I heard Barry's voicemail message, I thought it might be the case that Markham mentioned, and having listened to you, I think it is."

"So do I, and from what Barry's told me, it might be interesting, but how was your case?"

Unsurprisingly in my view, Marty was keen to change subjects and readily accepted my invitation to do so.

"Really interesting, James. Tell me what you think. The mobile home was on a permanent site and had been almost completely destroyed so that all that remained was the steel floor frame, the timber floor and the timber base frame of the walls."

"So, you could see the layout of the rooms?"

"Yes, and that was the first strange point I noticed. As is often the case, there were two external doors on the same side of the mobile home, and they were reached by individual cement block steps which were embedded into the ground. When I walked up one of the set of steps, I could see the space for the door in the timber base frame of the mobile home directly in front of me, but from the top of the other steps, I saw that the space for the other door in the base frame was displaced about half metre off centre."

"So, before the fire, you had to step sideways to enter through that door?"

"Yes."

"Go on."

"The mobile home was served by an underground cesspit, which was connected to the mobile home toilet by a plastic soil pipe routed above the ground. The second strange point is that a 2-metre section of the pipe was missing, and a 3-metre section of the pipe was on the ground next to the gap."

"I don't want to lower the tone of the conversation but was there any mess on the ground next to the open end of the section of soil pipe connected to the toilet?"

"No."

"Any other strange observations?" I said slowly.

"Yes, according to Barry McGee, the mobile home is described on the insurance policy as having a gas-fired boiler and a central-heating system but there were no radiators or any copper pipework or a boiler amongst the debris."

"And they would have survived the fire?"

"Of course – and the copper hot water tank did."

"What did the insured say about all this?"

"He said that the people in the locality couldn't be trusted and had stolen the boiler, all the copper pipework and the radiators after the fire."

"But they didn't steal the copper hot water tank? Were there caps on the ends of the hot water tank primary circuit pipes – the pipes that are normally connected to the boiler – or were those pipes open-ended?"

"Very good point, which is actually the third strange point. There were end caps fitted, and they had clearly been fitted before the fire because some burnt bitumen that had probably fallen from the destroyed roof was adhering to them."

"So, before the fire, the hot water storage tank couldn't have been connected to a boiler otherwise there wouldn't be end caps? The pipes should have been open-ended where, after the fire, the alleged thieves had cut or disconnected those pipes from the boiler."

"That's right."

"Also, the roof was felt-covered?"

"Probably. I can't think of any other explanation for the

burnt bitumen that was on the end caps, but the insured said the roof was tiled."

"It could have been lined with felt."

"They were only thirty or forty tiles amongst the debris, towards the front of the home."

"So, all the other tiles from the roof were stolen as well?" Marty chuckled.

"Did you find the identification plate?"

"No, did you expect me to?"

"No. I think the mobile home on the policy had a tiled roof and a central-heating system connected to a boiler, but I think that mobile home was moved off the site and replaced with an inferior mobile home before the fire. The replacement mobile home had no boiler, no radiators and no tiled roof, other than probably a cursory row of display tiles along the front elevation. Also, the distance between the two external doors in the replacement mobile home was about half a metre different from the distance between the two external doors in the original mobile home, so only one of the doorways of the replacement mobile home could be centred next to a fixed external set of steps.

"As to the toilet positions, the toilet of the replacement mobile home was one metre closer to the cesspit than the toilet of the original mobile home, so the soil pipe that connected the toilet of the original mobile home to the cesspit was too long to connect the toilet of the replacement mobile home, which was why a 3-metre section of soil pipe was removed and presumably placed next to the resultant 2-metre gap when the replacement mobile home was in position in the hope that the issue wouldn't be noticed. In fact, there's a lot of issues they hoped wouldn't be noticed."

"Well done; I agree."

"Were there any other mobile homes on the site?"

"Yes, but most of the residents I spoke to said they saw nothing. One resident said he heard a crackling noise at about four o'clock yesterday, and on looking outside, he saw a large fire in the kitchen of the incident mobile home. He saw the insured's pick-up truck wasn't parked outside so he called the fire brigade then called the insured on his mobile, and the insured returned fifteen minutes later."

"What did the insured say?"

"He lives there with his wife and three children. He tarmacs drives for a living, but he had no jobs yesterday afternoon so he was at home. He and his wife left the mobile home at about half past three to collect the children from school and go shopping. Shortly after four o'clock, they received the call from the neighbour. When they arrived home, the fire was going like a train and the fire brigade had just arrived. The insured thinks that they might have left a chip pan containing cooking oil heating on the hob."

"What, at half three in the afternoon?"

"He said they'd had a late lunch and that the hob might not have been switched off when the chips were cooked although the chip pan was taken off the hob when the chips were served and they ate lunch. He thinks that the chip pan was accidentally put back on the hob when they were checking the kitchen food cupboards before leaving."

"That's actually a plausible accidental cause but it doesn't detract from the fact it wasn't the mobile home on the policy."

"I agree. I am sure that the chip pan was left on a hob ring, which was on and that the cooking oil was ignited because although the bakelite hob control knobs were destroyed by the fire, all of the brass control knob spindles survived the fire and one was in the on position. I think also that the chip pan was deliberately left on a hob ring."

"You don't need to show that, of course, which would be almost impossible anyway. You only need to show that the mobile home wasn't the one on the policy for insurers to repudiate liability, which I think you can do."

"I agree."

"What did Markham have to say about all this?"

"Before I started the inspection, he said that there obviously wasn't much for me to do as the mobile home had been completely destroyed and everyone knew a chip pan had been left on the hob. He had a grin on his face like a big slice of watermelon when I showed him that one of the hob control spindles was in the on position. He didn't smile though when I pointed out the relative positions of the door openings and the steps and the gap in the soil pipe with the longer section of pipe next to the gap."

"Did you tell him what you thought of that evidence?"

"No, but I think he worked it out. He then got a bit matey. He said, 'There's not going to be any problem on this one, is there, Marty? It can just go through, can't it?' He then got shirty when I said, 'I can't say that, Harry.' He said, 'Look, this isn't that big. It's not one to have an argument about.' He then calmed down a little and said, 'Let's go down the pub and we can sort it out there.' I said that I couldn't, and he swore and asked, 'Why not?' I said, 'Harry, I can't.' And you know what he said? 'We're in the same golf club!'"

"Oh, dear."

"He didn't reply when I said, 'Bye,' before I drove off."

"He didn't say anything about the other case he went to yesterday when he first attended your mobile home fire?"

"Isn't that the one you're going to review?"

"On one level, it seems unlikely. He'd been doing that case for eight months, and there was no need for him to attend again yesterday, as far as I am aware. On the other hand, Harry met Simon at a scene in London this afternoon and told Simon he had only done two cases in Kent this year, both in Maidstone, and one of them was yours."

"In which case, he must have been at the case you're going to review, which is the only other one he's done in Maidstone. It's logical, as Spock would say."

"I can't understand why he would have gone to an eight-month-old case."

"If he thought we were going to be involved, he might have just gone to check that the scene hadn't been disturbed."

"I don't like that explanation. Firstly, it's not something a loss assessor would normally do, bearing in mind also he would have incurred time and expense to go there when he could have just called the insured and asked him whether the scene had been disturbed. Secondly, he didn't know for sure that we or anyone else was going to be instructed. And thirdly, from what he said to you – and Simon also – the indications he had were that we were going to be asked to review the case, which implies a consideration of the reports and photographs, without there necessarily being a scene inspection. Markham might actually kick up a fuss about us inspecting the scene. He will say it has already been inspected by Georgie of Willoughbys."

"But where does all this get you, James?"

"I don't know, but you can see why I'm uncomfortable."

"You need to make sure you inspect that scene and find out what Markham was doing there yesterday."

"I agree with you on that." We wished each other a good

weekend and ended the conversation.

The time was then half past five, and home and Jemima beckoned. Unfortunately, my pile of urgent cases was warming up. Top of the pile – and starting to glow in the dark – was a supplementary report which a lawyer had asked me to prepare on some points raised by the other side on a case heading rapidly to court. The case in question was a dwelling-house with a thatched roof, which had caught fire as a result of an ember being ejected from the chimney and falling onto the thatch.

I had been appointed by the insurers of the property, and the case was being run against the company that had installed the property's wood-burning stove about two years before the fire, on the basis that they had not increased the height of the original chimney to an appropriate level in accordance with building regulations. Such an increase in height was necessary because the flue fitted to the stove and routed up the inside of the original chimney would have had a much greater draw on the embers in the stove compared to the property's original open fire where cool air from the room would have been drawn into the chimney and provided a weak draw.

It followed that there was a much greater chance of larger embers being drawn up the stove flue then falling onto and igniting the thatch, as had evidently occurred in this case. Increasing the height of the chimney meant that there was more chance of the embers being dispersed to the atmosphere and if any embers did fall onto the thatch, it was likely that they would have burnt out before they did so, thereby greatly reducing the chances of ignition.

In my case, the installing company's insurer's investigator was an academic combustion scientist who had read an unscientific paper, which had been circulating in the fire investigation world for years and which claimed that thatch fires were caused not by embers but by heat conducting through the brick chimney and igniting the thatch. The basis of that paper appeared to be an observation (or assumption) that on many winter days – the season when stoves were predominantly used – the exterior of the thatch would be damp so could not be ignited by an ember. The paper described tests undertaken by the authors in which powerful gas-fired burners had been directed at a brick wall with the result that heat had conducted through the wall and ignited thatch placed against the other side of the wall, an arrangement that was unrepresentative of the relatively small amount of heat that passed through a chimney from a stove flue.

When I had originally read that paper, I was left with two related thoughts, which were that the authors had probably missed some evidence before propounding their theory on heat conduction through chimneys and that their tests had been shoehorned, possibly unwittingly, to prove the theory.

Subsequent analysis of thatched roof fire cases by Jacobs had shown that fires in thatched roofs almost always occurred when stoves were used following relatively long, dry, cold spells in winter, that is to say when the thatch was dry and susceptible to ignition by embers – the evidence missed by the authors of the heat conduction paper. Further scientific tests undertaken by the Fire Protection Association showed that the rate of heat conduction through brick chimneys carrying flues connected to stoves was so low that it was not a viable cause of thatch ignition.

I had encountered the confirmatory bias displayed by the authors of the heat conduction paper in various degrees of unwittingness in my career, although mainly in the context of theories being shoehorned to fit contradictory evidence, and I tried to make a point of checking whether there was any such bias when analysing problems. I thought that Marty's explanation for the second case that Markham attended in Maidstone yesterday contained an element of confirmatory bias in that it was a view formed by looking for an easy answer. I wondered also whether, like the heat conduction paper, there might be a better explanation.

I eventually dragged my mind back to the thatched roof fire case. The academic combustion scientist appointed by the installers of the stove and flue appeared to be unaware of the Fire Protection Association paper describing their tests, as all his views were based on the flawed conclusions in the heat conduction paper. It followed that I could easily counter the points he had made in his report, but there were so many to comment upon that by half past six, I had only made a little headway.

Barry McGee then called me on my mobile. "Hello, James, can you talk?" he asked.

"Yes, I'm still in the office, Barry."

"On Friday evening? You guys must be busy."

"You said it, Barry. How can I help?"

"I've been speaking to Markham, but he is in a foul mood and wasn't inclined to cooperate on the Mr Gerash case. He was bad-mouthing you on the Dagenham Glass case because Sheena has told him insurers will want to send your report to lawyers to provide an opinion on liability. He wanted to know what Georgie had said on the Dagenham Glass case, but I refused to tell him because he isn't representing my insured. He then started bad-mouthing Marty on the mobile home fire, saying there was clear evidence the chip pan had been left on the hob and that Marty was making ridiculous comments about the doorways, the soil pipe and the central-heating system. Marty has already called me and told me that in his view the mobile home on the policy was swapped for an inferior one and it's clearly a fraudulent attempt to obtain the insurance money. I told Markham the insurers of the mobile home wouldn't make a decision on liability until they had Marty's report, and I refused to tell him what Marty thought before I had received his report, which didn't help Markham's mood."

"So, what did he say on the Mr Gerash case?"

"He said that if you have been asked by insurers to review the evidence, you should only read the reports."

"I said insurers decide how the evidence is to be reviewed, and anyway, I would like someone to examine the clothing and shoes found by Isaac. He eventually agreed you can attend the scene – although I don't think he had much choice – but he said that neither he nor the insured would be there to answer questions and he asked you to confine your inspection to the clothes and shoes. He also said that this has gone on long enough, and he wants you to attend early next week."

"How do I gain access?"

"The ground-floor doors and windows have all been boarded over for security reasons, so you will have to remove the screws from the boarding over the front door. That door is locked but there is a key under a flowerpot in the outside porch."

"Okay, email me Georgie's and Isaac's reports, and I will read them on Monday, speak to Georgie on any queries and attend the scene on Tuesday."

"Thanks, James, will do. I've told Georgie you are now involved." We then wished each other a good weekend and ended the conversation.

I put my thatched roof fire file in my briefcase and went home.

Chapter 9

"Marty is getting tiresome," Jemima said as we enjoyed a dinner of seafood risotto, which she had cooked exquisitely, and shared a bottle of Pinot Grigio. "His explanation for missing Barry's call was far too detailed," she continued. "And for goodness sake, he must realise that he is fooling no one if Selena rings in sick when he is doing a case at short notice in Kent. It's almost as if he is flaunting his affair."

"Perhaps he is in a strange way. He wants to hide it and simultaneously show off, but I don't know; I'm not a psychiatrist."

"If he's not careful, he will come unstuck badly."

"What do you think of Markham?"

"I don't like the sound of him at all. Too many of his clients seem to be attempting to commit fraud, and he must be aware of that, but he persists with pleading accidental causes, which ultimately will fail."

"What he is doing is not illegal. In the Dagenham Glass case, he has appointed an ex-fire officer investigator who will say the fire was started accidentally, and Markham will say he is simply attempting to obtain the best outcome for his client, as is stated on his business card. As you know, there is a very high burden of proof for an allegation of fraud, even in a civil case, so his efforts against insurers and me might not be in vain. I am more concerned about how he seems to turn up on cases when he might be expected to be elsewhere. Marty thinks he rides his luck."

"You see him here; you see him there. You don't see him here; you don't see him there," sang Jemima, then continued, "which is reflected in the split persona of respectable golf club member and weaselly loss assessor, exemplified also by wildly different attire. Sounds like a dangerous Dr Jekyll and Mr Hyde character to me. Perhaps he knows he's one and wants to be the other."

"Which way round?"

Jemima hesitated, then said, "On reflection, perhaps he doesn't know. When he is being one, he might look forward to escaping to the other. But I want you to take care, darling James. From what you've said, he has a tendency to turn nasty if things don't go his way, and if you give him a chance, he wouldn't hesitate to harm you." Jemima looked at me intently.

I got up, walked round to her, kissed her and held her close. "I am taking him very seriously, which is why we're discussing him, even on a Friday evening."

"Good," she said, kissing me, "but as it's Friday evening, let's now try to relax."

Relaxing involved washing up after the meal, curling up together on the sofa to watch a comedy CD then writhing together in bed.

Saturday appeared as a gently increasing glow in our sleepy contentment. I slipped myself out of bed early and showered because this Saturday, like many Saturdays, meant going to the races, and as always, I wanted to study the form over breakfast. I left the flat with Jemima sleeping soundly, walked along to the shops next to Archway tube station, purchased the *Racing Post* and a newspaper then went into my favourite local café.

Two young women greeted me with their ready Saturday

smiles and sparkling eyes. Samantha and Julie made amazing cappuccinos and fabulous bacon butties. They served them with friendliness and a little banter.

"Morning, James," said Samantha.

"Morning, Samantha. Morning, Julie."

"The usual?" asked Julie.

"Of course," I replied, returning their smiles.

"Very smart, James, must be Ascot," said Samantha.

"You know me too well."

"Well enough for you to take Julie and me one day?"

"My wife wouldn't approve."

"We'd keep it quiet, James," said Julie.

"Find yourselves a boyfriend each, and I'll take you all."

"There's a promise," said Samantha.

"I would, actually."

"We're working on the boyfriends, but we will be there with you in spirit today," said Julie.

"One day, when you think we're here, we'll just turn up unannounced and ask for tips," said Samantha.

A la Markham, I thought but said, "The best one is 'don't bet too much'."

"James," continued Samantha, "you'll give us proper tips, won't you? You do well!"

"Only fifty per cent of the time, but if you promise to only bet a little, I will give you proper tips."

"I knew I would persuade you, James."

I thought that Samantha and Julie, both being naturally pretty and curvaceous, could easily persuade a lot of men to do what they wanted, even the married ones. They started serving new customers whilst I settled down to breakfast and analysed the data in the *Racing Post*.

I had invented a handicap system which involved carrying out a simple calculation for each horse based on the historical racing data contained in the *Racing Post*. It often took me four or five hours to analyse a seven-race meeting but I enjoyed it, even though the ratings I obtained had limited meaning. On successful days, I balanced the ratings – without straying too far from them – with considerations of whether the distance, course and state of the ground were suitable for each horse, whilst taking into account also that some horses could make dramatic improvements when they were young. Like investigating fires, it was necessary to understand what was real evidence – factual-based data – and what was worthless group-think – lots of punters often blindly following the view of a single newspaper columnist and heavily influencing the odds.

An hour later, I had analysed three races, and sipping the last of my coffee, I waved Samantha and Jane goodbye then made my way back to the flat.

Jemima had showered and dressed and was in the kitchen making tea and toast. I gave her a kiss and a hug and placed the newspaper on the table for her. "What are your plans for the day?" I asked.

"Some early Christmas shopping in Oxford Street."

"Oh, no!" I liked Christmas but disliked the shopping, as Jemima knew.

"Oh, yes! There's no need to think too hard, James. I'm drawing up a list for you to consider, as usual."

"You're so kind." She was. As well as a reasonably extensive selection for herself, Jemima's gift list would also include suggestions for our respective small families.

"My chicken in white wine sauce this evening?" I continued, referring to a meal I had cooked on Tuesday evening and placed in the fridge.

"Perfect. See you later."

We kissed goodbye and I travelled to Ascot via the tube and train, with the time passing quickly as I continued my analysis and marked up the *Racing Post* with my ratings.

I arrived about an hour before the first race. I was an annual member at Ascot, so I entered the cavernous main stand and made my way via the huge Up escalator and an internal gallery walkway to the members' bar in the stand's premier – King Edward VII – area, which was on the second floor, nodding to the bowler-hatted staff who were checking badges at the escalators' entrances and exits and at the doorway to the bar itself.

Marcel, the bar manager, was grey-haired but an indeterminate age and maintained a largely expressionless countenance, with only a flick of an eyebrow, a gentle nod or a subtle wink betraying any emotion and sometimes being the only form of communication. He seemed to know everybody and everything about everything, in part because the open, upper sections of the members' bar boundary constructions allowed him to see what was happening in the adjacent sections of the King Edward VII.

I often wondered if Marcel was on wheels when he moved around the members' bar, collecting glasses whilst simultaneously acknowledging a multitude of people. He was currently behind the bar counter and served me my usual Cola with ice and lemon. I didn't like drinking alcohol during the day and positively avoided it at the races.

"Bayleaf in the fourth each way is the best today, Marcel," I said as he, with a lightly arched eyebrow, next handed me my crisps and sandwiches – also usual – and I swiped my credit card. Marcel glanced briefly at me with smiling eyes and turned effortlessly to the next customer.

I wandered outside to the members' exclusive viewing seats and walked down some access steps to the lowest row, which was still very high up and provided almost a bird's-eye view of the track, the King Edward VII lawn next to the finishing straight and the bookmakers' pitches that bounded both ends of the lawn. I was looking for my favourite bookmaker who had authority to provide enhanced odds to some regular punters, which included me. After scanning the pitches for about ten seconds, I saw the bookmaker setting up the electronic odds board for a pitch on the left side of the lawn. I then nearly fell over the safety barrier and into the narrow safety net because standing on the lawn close to the bookmaker was Harry Markham in full spiv regalia.

I was transfixed. Markham was chatting expensively with three other men, one of whom I recognised and whose presence there with Markham surprised me but only slightly. I was reasonably sure I had never previously seen Markham's other two companions, and I immediately decided I wanted a photograph of them all although without them seeing me.

I walked slowly back up the steps and into the members' bar where Marcel was operating in full radar mode so I quickly caught his eye. His waltz over to me around the people standing in the room would have won high marks on *Strictly Come Dancing* for subtlety and style.

"I need a favour doing, Marcel, but I will understand it if you decline."

Marcel nodded delicately.

"There are four racegoers standing together at the left side of the lawn. One of them looks like a nastier version of Walker from *Dad's Army*. I would like a close-up photograph taken of them on my mobile, but I don't want them to see me."

Marcel nodded deftly then walked outside and down the steps to the safety barrier from where he looked down and to the left. He then returned to me and glanced at my mobile phone, which I was holding. I slipped it into his hand, and Marcel made his way back to the bar counter where I saw him speak briefly to one of the temporary staff. He then picked up one of the complimentary *Racing Posts* from the bar counter and left the members' bar via the doorway leading to the internal gallery walkway.

I walked back down the external steps to the safety barrier and almost missed Marcel when a few minutes later he appeared on the left side of the King Edward VII lawn. He had taken off his barman's jacket and bow tie and was wearing a raincoat. He was also reading the *Racing Post*, and walking slowly towards the bookmakers' pitches; he looked every inch the professional punter. Other racegoers were in that area, mainly looking at the odds on the bookmakers' boards, but some people in small groups were taking photographs of each other as souvenirs of their day out.

I had to admire Marcel. He firstly stood to one side but behind a young woman who was taking a photograph of a family group that happened to be standing in front of Markham and his companions. Marcel then placed the *Racing Post* under his arm, raised my mobile phone and took a photograph of the Markham group who no doubt thought he was taking a photograph of the family who were hiding the young woman from their view. The family probably thought – correctly – that Marcel was taking a photograph of a group behind them.

A few minutes later, Marcel was back in the members' bar

wearing his barman's jacket and bow tie. He weaved his way through the crowd in the room and handed me my mobile phone whilst walking past with a tray of drinks for other people balanced on his other hand. I then made my way down an escalator to the ground floor and stood at a doorway, which provided a view of the left side of the King Edward VII lawn.

Markham's group had moved away from the bookmakers' pitches, presumably having placed their bets, and had walked down to the finishing rail in the area close to the centre of the lawn. They were far enough away not to notice me if I stood next to the bookmakers' pitches, particularly through the gathering crowd of racegoers on the lawn.

I walked to my favourite bookmaker.

"Good afternoon, James," said Pauline, young, beautiful, intelligent and friendly but well-armed with barriers that I had never tried to breach. Others I suspect had tried – and failed.

"Good afternoon, Pauline," I replied and gave her my bets, a single bet to win and two each way in the 10-runner first race, all small bets, as always. I enjoyed analysing the races, but my system was not perfect as it did not take into account all the variables that can affect a horse's performance, so my bets were designed to ensure I never lost much. Conversely, I rarely won large amounts.

"Pauline," I said after she gave me my tickets.

"Yes, James," she replied matter of factly, the first stage of a barrier being raised.

"A short time ago, there was a guy dressed like a second-hand car salesman on steroids standing near your pitch. You don't know who he is, do you?"

Pauline relaxed. "I don't know his name. He's been coming to the races fairly frequently during the past three years and bets with all the bookmakers. He used to dress more soberly but the past year or so he has dressed similarly to today." Pauline always chose her words carefully.

"Thanks," and knowing that Pauline knew my day job, I explained, "I'm reasonably sure I've seen him on some of my cases, and I don't want to bump into him here."

"He's usually on the lawn, so you'll need to take care."

"Thanks, Pauline, I will."

I spent the remainder of the afternoon as usual, shuttling between the members' bar viewing seats and Pauline's pitch. I kept a beady eye on Markham's whereabouts, and thankfully, I managed to avoid him. I reflected that I had been lucky not to encounter him on previous visits, and on checking the photograph taken by Marcel, I noticed that neither Markham nor his companions were wearing annual member's badges. Like the vast majority of the King Edward VII racegoers, they had purchased day tickets so were only wearing day badges. I would not be meeting them in the members' bar, but I needed to keep an eye out that they did not walk along the internal walkway and look into the bar through the open parts of the boundary constructions.

My selections won three of the seven races at short prices, and I had two each way successes including Bayleaf, which finished second at 40 to 1 to a hot favourite in the 15-runner fourth race. After that race, I walked into the members' bar to check whether Marcel had backed Bayleaf each way. A flicker of a wink and a narrow smile indicated he had. Every time I attended Ascot, I only gave Marcel one tip, the best horse from my analysis, and Bayleaf was the tenth consecutive successful tip, so I understood Marcel's readiness to do me a favour in taking the photograph. I did, however, wonder how much he was betting on my tips.

Jemima's eyes widened in genuine horror when I told her that Markham had been at the races. They widened even further when she saw Markham's photograph. "It's not often that someone looks just like you expected them to. If anything, he looks worse. Why was he there?"

I told her what Pauline had told me. I also told her my views on his companions.

"You may be right, but you haven't got any proof."

"Difficult to prove, but I'll have a think about it."

"Don't spend all weekend thinking about it." We both knew that I would.

I started off with good intentions though. I did all the preparation for the chicken and white wine sauce dinner, which we both enjoyed, and I made more than a token effort to show interest in the shopping trip: not too busy and reasonably successful. We then lay together on the sofa in contented laziness watching a film.

I spent Sunday morning sitting at the kitchen table determinedly finishing a dictated draft of my supplementary report on the thatched roof fire, during which time Jemima played some lovely music on the piano in the lounge. In the afternoon, we firstly walked around St James' Park looking at the various birds because Jemima knew I was a keen birdwatcher. We then went to London Zoo because Jemima knew I was interested in wild animals. It was her idea to take my mind off work. It was not successful.

At the zoo, I wondered about the symptoms of paranoia. I watched a cockerel strutting around in front of hens, and I thought of Marty. I also watched a chimpanzee throwing goodness knows what at members of the public, and I thought of Isaac. Finally, when watching some gibbons scratching each other's backs, I thought of Markham.

Chapter 10

On Monday I arrived at the office at seven thirty again and left the memory chip with my dictated supplementary report on Mavis' desk for formalising. No one else was in so I logged onto Jacobs' computer system, accessed the drive storing the photographs and opened Marty's folder, something which was not prevented by Jacobs' software. Strictly, however, out of courtesy, I should have asked Marty's permission before doing so.

I looked through Marty's photographs of the mobile home case, and all the evidence was clearly recorded: the gap in the soil pipe, the offset doorways, the caps on the hot water tank primary circuit connectors and the small number of roof tiles. I was looking for something else, and I could not be certain it would be there, but I did eventually find it and it made me smile.

I closed Marty's folder and the drive then accessed the Mr Gerash case emails with Georgie's and Isaac's reports as attachments, which Barry had sent me on Friday evening and which I had resisted reading over the weekend. Georgie's report eliminated almost all of the accidental causes, including two that Barry and I had not discussed but I had wondered about since our conversation on Friday.

Firstly, some high-end decorating was carried out using scumble-glaze paints mixed with linseed oil, which slowly oxidises generating heat. Jacobs had encountered cases in which decorators using scumble-glaze paints had neglected to clear rolled-up cotton cleaning rags from properties, and the heat generated by the oxidation of the linseed oil contaminating the rags had caused the temperature of the rags to increase to the ignition temperature of the cotton during the night, in part due to the insulating effect of the rags preventing the heat from dissipating to the atmosphere. In the Mr Gerash case, however, the decorators had said they had only used emulsion and gloss paints, and Georgie had found no scumble-glaze paints or linseed oil at the property, so a cause involving those materials could be discounted.

Georgie had also examined all the halogen heater components and the remains of the fixed sockets, lights and wiring in the hall. The only evidence of electrical arcing she had found comprised some small beads of once-molten copper close to the middle of the heater lead's exposed conductors. Georgie had firstly concluded that the heater lead was live, and she confirmed this by checking the plug socket switch, which was on.

Georgie had further concluded, correctly in my view, that the lead had probably been draped over the bags of waste materials piled in the hall in order to connect the heater to the plug socket and that the fire involving those bags of waste materials had first burnt the insulation from the lead at about the midpoint thereby causing the exposed conductors to touch and arc at that position. Georgie had concluded from the pattern of fire damage and the position of the arcing on the heater lead – and again, I agreed – that the fire had probably started amongst the bags of waste materials piled in the hall.

Georgie had stated that the fire could have been started deliberately by someone with access to keys who had entered the property after Mr Gerash had left and had applied a naked flame, such as a lit match, to the bags of waste materials. Georgie's examination of the heater components had, however, shown that when the fire occurred, the integral power switch of the heater was on. On this basis, she had further concluded that the heater was operating and the fire could have been started as a result of the bags having been deliberately piled up against the front of the heater before Mr Gerash vacated the property at 1730 hours on the day of the fire.

Georgie's final conclusion was that she could not discount the possibility that the fire resulted from some of the bags of waste materials having collapsed accidentally against the front grille of the heater due to Mr Gerash slamming the door as he left the property. That was a critical conclusion, and having read Georgie's report, I did agree with her, as I had said to Barry McGee.

Georgie's photographs, which were appended to her report, included views of what appeared to be a burnt pile of clothing and some shoes on the remains of the bed in the main bedroom, but the pile was partly hidden by some large, burnt roof timbers that had collapsed onto the bed. It would have been necessary to employ assistance, such as demolition contractors, to remove the timbers in order to access the pile, and as the contents of the pile were unlikely to have provided any evidence on the cause of the fire – that had started amongst the bags of waste materials in the hall – I fully understood why Georgie had not requested insurers to incur the expense of removing the timbers when she had attended the scene shortly after the fire.

Isaac's report was poorly written, but in fairness, it quickly got to the point. After a brief resume of the circumstances and a short description of the fire damage from which it was clear Isaac had not examined the halogen heater retained by Georgie –

although he did not state that explicitly – Isaac concluded that in his professional opinion, "the fire had started accidentally as a result of the bags of waste materials falling against the front of the halogen heater in the hall when Mr Gerash slammed the door as he left. The heater, which had been inadvertently left switched on, had ignited a smoulder in the waste materials and the smoulder had developed to flames later in the evening."

I had no doubt that Markham had told Isaac that this was Mr Gerash's explanation for the fire and Isaac had written his report to support that view. In one sense, however, his report was effective because the absence of any discussion of other causes would leave a non-questioning reader with the impression that the collapse of some bags of waste materials against the heater was the only plausible cause, and I could understand how a lawyer appointed by insurers would advise them to pay up, bearing in mind also that Georgie had stated she could not discount such a cause.

I was annoyed and slightly disturbed by Isaac's first reference to the items that Barry had mentioned – the Armani shirts, Boss suits, other items of clothing, shoes and training shoes – which Isaac described in the third-person past perfect: "The items that had been found piled on the bed in the main bedroom had been laid out in rows in a ground-floor room."

On my first reading of that sentence, I was left with the impression that the items had been removed from the bed and placed in the ground-floor room before Isaac's attendance. I did appreciate that the sentence might have been poorly drafted and many, perhaps most, readers might conclude that as Isaac had written the report, it was he who had found the items on the bed and placed them in the ground-floor room, but at no point did his report explicitly state that he was involved in either action.

Also, there was no photograph, like the photograph in Georgie's report, showing the roof timbers lying on top of the pile of items on the bed. Further, although only a selection of the photographs Isaac had taken was appended to his report, none of those photographs showed any of the items before they were removed from the main bedroom. The only photograph of the bed that was included in the report essentially showed mattress springs on a steel frame, so that photograph had been taken after the pile of items had been removed.

I decided to call Georgie.

"Morning, James, I understand you've been asked to review the Mr Gerash case."

"Morning, Georgie, I have, and I've just finished reading your report and Isaac's report. I haven't got any issue with your report."

"Would you have excavated the pile of items on the bed if, like me, you had attended a few days after the fire and long before there was a suspicion of an exaggerated claim?"

"No, you were unlucky with that."

"Thank you."

"What do you think of Isaac's report?"

"Superficial, case pleading. Neither Barry nor I knew Markham had appointed Isaac until after Markham had sent Isaac's report to Barry, so now it will appear that Isaac has been very thorough by excavating the debris on the bed and that I wasn't, even though he attended the scene in part to assist with the contents claim so was always going to look at the items on the bed. It was underhand of him not to inform me he was going to the scene and, in particular, not to give me an opportunity to excavate the items on the bed. Also, he formed a view on the heater without inspecting the halogen heater that I had retained."

"Interesting that Isaac's report never actually states he excavated the pile of items on the bed."

"Doesn't it?"

"No, it states that the items that *had been* found on the bed and *had been* laid out in rows in a ground-floor room. It doesn't state that *he* found them on the bed. Also, none of his photographs show any of the items in the main bedroom. One interpretation of his report could be that the items were removed from the main bedroom by someone else and placed in the ground-floor room before Isaac attended. That is actually how his text reads. That interpretation would of course fail if Isaac had included a photograph showing the un-excavated pile of items on the bed with the roof timbers on top of the pile when he attended – as you did – but there was no such photograph in his report."

"I think you may be reading too much into it, James. Isaac's writing isn't as precise as Jacobs and Willoughbys expect in their reports, and he probably just included photographs showing the critical evidence, the Armani and Boss labels in particular, which unfortunately, hit the target."

"I think I will still ask him if the items had been removed from the bed before he attended, but I will play him at his game, so I won't call him until after I've been to the scene. At the moment, Markham doesn't want anyone else to attend when I'm there as he doesn't want to give me any help, and I don't want to say anything to Isaac that might cause Markham to change his mind."

"When are you going?"

"Tomorrow."

"Can you call me after you've been?"

"Yes, I'll let you know how I get on."

"Thanks, James, and good luck."

The morning had evaporated, and when I finished the call to Georgie, Mavis came into my office with a smile and informed me that she had formalised the thatched roof report and it was ready for checking. It was shortly after half past twelve, when everyone usually went to lunch, so I decided to go out to buy some sandwiches and check the report whilst eating lunch in my office.

On a whim, before going to the sandwich shop, I decided to look in at Marty's office to see if he was there and, if so, whether he had any further information on Markham's golf club activities. I went up to Marty's office, knocked on the door, opened it and just managed to see Marty and Selena leaping apart from a warm embrace.

"That'll be fine; just type it this afternoon," said Marty to Selena awkwardly, with a swivel-eyed look at his desk. Selena took her cue and picked up what was clearly a blank sheet of paper from Marty's desk whilst turning a deep shade of crimson. She then walked out of Marty's office with her eyes looking at the floor.

So they were having a kiss and cuddle when they thought everyone was at lunch, and they will not be happy that I have uncovered that plot line.

Marty decided to brazen it out by maintaining a slab face and leaving me to say something. I decided to say nothing about what I had seen, and I was especially determined not to give him a false plaudit, such as a nod or a wink, so I simply said, "I was wondering if you'd had a chance to enquire about Markham's other golf club memberships."

"I was just about to come and see you, James," replied Marty, without a flicker of irony. "He cancelled his previous golf club membership when he became a member at the Imperial, and he's not a member of any other club."

"I'm not surprised; neither of us thought he was going to another golf club AGM last Tuesday. By the way, I'm going to that case in Maidstone tomorrow for Barry McGee."

"Where we think Markham was on the day he first went to my mobile home fire?"

"I'm not convinced on that explanation either, but I'll keep an eye out for anything Markham may have done recently at the scene. How is your mobile home report coming along? Barry told me on Friday that he informed Markham the insurers won't make a decision on liability until they have your report."

"I'm on with it, and Barry is pressing me for it."

"Barry said Markham was in a foul mood what with my Dagenham Glass case, your mobile home case and now me being appointed to review the case I'm going to in Maidstone tomorrow."

"That's Markham's problem."

"The foul mood is probably the least of his problems. There is a huge risk that the Dagenham Glass and mobile home cases will be repudiated, in which case Markham will earn nothing on those cases. He is also not out of the woods yet on the Maidstone case I'm going to tomorrow."

"All his problems."

"Hopefully, his foul mood doesn't turn nasty or they might become our problems. He's already been awkward on my Maidstone case."

"He's all bluster. He'll calm down soon."

I did not think Marty was right, but I did not pursue the point, and after explaining I was going to buy some sandwiches, I left him to reflect on his interrupted tryst.

In the afternoon, I checked my supplementary report on the

thatched roof fire then emailed it to the client. I also reflected briefly on interruptions in general and their consequences. One of the interruptions concerned a file on my desk that was in amber alert mode and involved a fire that had started at the integral on/off (power) switch of a television, about ten months after the television had been purchased new from a well-known manufacturer with a reputation for quality.

The owner of the television – and the luxurious incident property – had been watching the television in the lounge one evening and at some point had gone into the bathroom. Whilst in the bathroom, the power to the property was interrupted, as evidenced by the lights going out. Upon investigating – in the dark – the owner re-entered the lounge and observed flames at the lower-right corner of the television, where the power switch was located. The owner had immediately vacated the property and called the fire brigade who had attended quickly but were unable to prevent the fire from causing severe soot damage to the expensive contents of the property.

The fire had occurred only a month ago, and I had carried out the investigation for the building and contents insurers who had sent my report to a firm of top London lawyers for an opinion as to whether they could recover their outlay from the television manufacturers. My examination of the television had revealed evidence of localised melting characteristic of a progressive electrical fault on the copper conducting components of the power switch of the television. In my view, the fault had eventually generated sufficient heat to cause the plastic components of the switch to ignite. The fire had then developed, and the sensitive electrical trip switch of the property had quickly operated thereby interrupting the power supply.

Given that the television was purchased new and that the

owner had informed me there had been no previous problems with the appliance, I concluded that the fire was most likely caused by a manufacturing defect at the switch.

The lawyer had sent me an email, which made it clear she was not impressed. She said I had not considered "customer abuse" and was surprised that I thought a fire would occur in such a reputable manufacturer's appliance, bearing in mind also that there had been no previous instance of fires involving that model of television, which had been extensively advertised as technologically advanced when it was launched.

I decided to call the lawyer. "What was the 'customer abuse' you had in mind?"

"Well, someone could have accidentally knocked the television onto the floor and damaged the power switch whilst doing housework."

I took a deep breath before answering. "As shown in my photographs, the television was secured to a heavy support base, which was in turn positioned in the centre of the top surface of a large cabinet, so it is extremely unlikely that the television could have been dislodged onto the floor, particularly as it was restrained by virtue of its power, aerial and CD cable attachments. Also, the floor was covered in a deep pile carpet, which would have cushioned any fall."

"Oh... but it still can't be ruled out."

"That's not the point. In a civil case, the court is concerned with 'balance of probabilities', and there is no realistic chance that the judge would find that the power switch was damaged as a result of the television having been dislodged onto the floor."

"I don't need a lecture on the niceties of civil cases."

I took a very large deep breath and decided not to say that it was she who had suggested that not being able to rule out the possibility of dislodgment was a relevant point. Instead, I said, "I don't agree with your argument that because the manufacturer is respected for quality, a court will deduce that a manufacturing defect could not have caused the fire. There have been numerous examples of international companies with a high reputation making errors and being successfully sued in court for the resultant losses. Not so long ago, some high-profile German car manufacturers were successfully sued for an emissions scandal involving their diesel engines."

"That involved thousands of customers. There have been no other fires caused by this model of television."

"Following that argument, there would never be a first time for anything."

"What?"

"Well, you say that this fire wasn't caused by a manufacturing defect because there are no other known fires involving this television. Suppose next month, Jacobs receive instructions on a fire starting at one of these model televisions, with evidence of localised melting at the power switch, would you say that fire could have been caused by a manufacturing defect?"

"Well, of course, because that would be the second one."

"But from your perspective, it would not be the second one. It would be the first one because you say this one was not caused by a manufacturing defect at the television. You could only say the one next month was the second one if you were to accept you were wrong to dismiss this one because it was the first one."

"Are you trying to be funny?"

"No, I am pointing out the flaw in your logic. Bear in mind also that this television was purchased new shortly after the model was released onto the market and the owner watched the television for long periods each day, so it would not be surprising that it was the first television to exhibit signs of a progressive fault caused by a manufacturing defect. Jacobs of course, being the primary fire investigators in the country, would be expected to investigate fires caused by the first appliance to catch fire due to a manufacturing defect, which we have done on previous occasions involving other manufacturers."

A long silence. Just before I was about to ask if she was still there, she said, "I would like you to put this in writing."

"Fine, I will say exactly what I have said now."

"I look forward to receiving your supplementary report as soon as possible."

"No problem, have a good day."

She put the telephone down without replying.

I wondered whether it had been worth calling the lawyer. On balance I thought it was because, hopefully, it would motivate her to think more deeply about the case before receiving my written thoughts. Her silent pause suggested she had started to think properly. Unfortunately, I often encountered people who did not consider whether their first thought (a television been knocked onto the floor by housework) was technically plausible and who also were influenced by prejudice (a manufacturer with a reputation for quality could not produce a defective item).

I spent the remainder of the afternoon dictating a supplementary report to the lawyer. Mavis quickly formalised it, and I checked and emailed it to the lawyer before leaving the office and going home.

Jemima said, "It's a good job you didn't go into Marty's office ten minutes later."

"I hope you're not right, but if you are, it would be

unacceptable. Their affair is already affecting whether he takes cases on, where he does them and when, which I think is a problem."

"Are you going to speak to him about it?"

"I'll probably discuss it with the other partners."

Jemima changed the subject, "Georgie was unlucky with the items on the bed, but she missed the grammatical nuances in Isaac's report."

"Mind you, we don't know if I'm right on that," I replied.

"I think you are. It's the sort of thing you notice, get your teeth into and people say you are wrong about, but then you are proved right in the end."

"You should go into PR."

"You are modest, but it helps you because you never claim you've solved something until you've found supporting evidence."

"You observe people well, as I've told you many times. You should go into personnel."

"PR, personnel, not enough intellectual challenge. I like the legal profession because insurance cases do actually involve a lot of character analysis."

"The full spectrum of the human condition and amplified when there is money at stake."

"Take care with Markham."

"I am."

Chapter 11

The rain that had fallen through the open roof of Mr Gerash's property during the previous eight months had resulted in mould forming in all of the upstairs rooms. More worryingly, the floors in the upstairs rooms sagged when I walked on them.

I carried out the inspection of the property whilst referring to the photographs in Georgie's and Isaac's reports, which I opened on my mobile phone. The light of my torch picked out no remaining helpful physical evidence in the hall, as Georgie had excavated and cleared the debris there after removing the heater. Nonetheless, my overall analysis of the pattern of fire damage to the building reinforced my view that Georgie's view on origin was correct.

I turned to Isaac's report. By comparing the interior of the property with the photographs in Isaac's report, it appeared that nothing had been altered between Isaac's inspection about a month ago and my attendance, which raised the question as to what Markham had done if he had visited on the day of the mobile home fire.

I stood in the doorway of the main bedroom. The rusting, steel bed frame and mattress springs in the otherwise empty room might have won a modern art prize but from a forensic perspective were stark and challenging. I eventually moved to the ground-floor room where the burnt clothing items that had been removed from the bed were laid out in rows, as described by Isaac. Most of the clothing was severely fire-damaged and yielded no useful evidence.

I checked the various labels that remained and looked especially at the Armani and Boss labels. I wondered if the labels were fake and compared them with real and fake labels that I found on the internet, but despite having some doubts concerning one or two labels, there was no positive evidence that allowed me to conclude any of the labels were fake. I also looked at the serial numbers on the labels, but the few that were still visible were not obviously helpful. I recorded and photographed them for possible further investigation.

One of the labels, a wash label, was attached to a partly burnt summer jacket sold by a well-known high-street manufacturer, and this jacket was in one of the photographs in Isaac's report. The serial number was on the underside of the wash label, and upon lifting this label to photograph the number, I noticed that underneath there was a smaller, brown label that was apparently blank. This latter label caused me to pause because I could not understand why a manufacturer would incur the expense of fitting a garment with a label displaying no information.

A closer inspection of the small label revealed that the fire had destroyed part of one corner, but the flame had progressed no further, leaving the remainder of the label scorched, hence the brown colour. Given this evidence, it seemed likely that there was some information on the small label but that it was masked by the scorching. Shining my torch on the small label from different angles revealed nothing, most likely because the yellow light provided too much of a glare, which itself provided a masking effect. Therefore, I took the jacket outside and slowly turned the small label in the thin, white, winter light. At one position, the following became visible on the label: 05/22. By an effort of considerable contortion with my camera, I managed to obtain a photograph showing these digits. There was no other information on the small label to indicate the meaning of the digits which occupied almost the entire label.

These observations puzzled me for several reasons. Firstly, the purpose of the digits was not clear although obviously they must mean something to at least some people somewhere. Secondly, the label displaying the digits was small and was under the larger label, an arrangement which appeared to be an attempt to hide the digits, but the digits themselves were large so they would be readily apparent to people who knew where they were and what they meant. The digits looked a little like a batch number, but I could not understand why a manufacturer or retailer would display the batch number on an individual label, particularly as it was usual for a batch number to be either part of the serial number (which was on the underside of the wash label) or displayed on the garment packaging.

The questions were raised as to who were the select people who knew where the digits were and what they meant? Why did these people seemingly need to see the digits easily? Why also had the manufacturer or retailer tried to either hide the digits or their meaning from other people, like me, presumably the general public – or possibly even disguise the digits as a batch number? Most importantly, what did the digits mean?

I appreciated that by this stage, I was probably overthinking the issue, but I had found little else of interest at the scene; so after securing the property, I drove home thinking long and hard about the digits on the label.

I told Jemima what I thought. She went to her wardrobe and found two garments she had purchased from the same retailer as the summer jacket. Both of Jemima's garments, like the summer jacket, were fitted with small labels positioned under the larger wash label and both small labels displayed two pairs of digits separated by a '/'.

Jemima said that her recollections were a little vague, but my explanation could account for the digits on her garments. "What are you going to do about it?" she asked.

"Speak to the retailer."

"Are you going to spend the rest of the evening thinking about it?"

"Not if you tempt me."

She tempted me.

Chapter 12

On the following morning, Wednesday, it only took a couple of telephone calls and a few repeat explanations before I spoke to a senior manager in the summer jacket retailer's security department. She asked me to email her my photographs of the summer jacket and the label, which I did immediately. She paused while she looked at the photographs on her laptop then said she would call me back shortly.

Half an hour later, she called me. "The digits on the small label are the date of manufacture and are part of our anti-fraud procedures. When a garment is returned to a shop, the retail assistant lifts the wash label and checks that the date on the small label is consistent with the date on the receipt presented by the customer," an explanation that dealt with all my queries concerning the digits.

In the Mr Gerash case, the fire was about eight months ago, March 2022, but the date of manufacture of the summer jacket was 05/22, May 2022.

The senior security manager further advised me that this particular style of summer jacket had been manufactured in China and was first advertised in the retailer's 2022 Summer Catalogue, with the first batch of jackets arriving in the UK in June 2022 and being sold in their shops from the end of June. She confirmed to me she would be prepared to sign a statement containing the information she had provided, and I told her I was very grateful for her assistance.

I had told Jemima that I thought the digits were the date of manufacture, and she had said that the digits on the small labels of her two garments could be manufacturing dates given her recollections of when she had purchased them. I had not, however, known for certain that the digits were the manufacturing date and if so why that date was being displayed on the small label, but now I did know the answers to both these points. More importantly, I knew the summer jacket had been purchased, partly burned and planted in Mr Gerash's property after the fire and more specifically between June 2022 and Isaac's attendance a month ago.

I called Barry McGee and told him my findings. He swore.

"You do of course know there is case law that if one part of a claim is shown to be fraudulent then the entire claim fails," I said.

"I do," said Barry, "so after we've spoken, I'll call the insurers' lawyers so that they can contact the retailer's senior security manager about drafting her statement. Can you send me a prelim report ASAP?"

"I can. Also, I've told Georgie I'd let her know my findings. Are you content with that?"

"I'll call her and give her brief details. I'll also impress upon her that no one else must know about this at present. I want this kept under wraps until the lawyers have considered it."

"One other point, Barry, is that I was concerned about Isaac's report. He wrote some of it with detached expressions which suggested to me that the clothing and shoes had been removed from the bed in the main bedroom and placed in the downstairs room before his attendance, but he did not state that explicitly. I was going to ask him to provide me with all of his photographs to see if there was one showing the items on the bed.

I could also ask him outright if the bed had been cleared before he got there. I appreciate you might not want me to raise these questions with Isaac yet because you don't want to alert him or, more importantly, Markham, to me having found a problem with Mr Gerash's claim. It might, however, be worthwhile raising these questions with the insurer's lawyers."

"Yes, I agree, don't speak to Isaac. I will advise the lawyers of the issues. Do you think Isaac knew the clothing had been planted?"

"I don't think he was told that, but I suspect when he attended the scene, he observed the bed had been cleared and he felt uncomfortable. I suspect also he was told the clearance had been done so that he wouldn't have to go to the trouble of removing the large timbers from the bed. Assuming I am right, he should have stated clearly in his report that the clothing and shoes had been removed from the bed before he attended but he did not. I think he finessed his wording to hide the clearance because he thought it would help his client if it appeared that the bed had not been disturbed prior to his inspection. The implication though is that he was aware the clearance would raise the question of clothing having been planted, so an attempt to cover up the clearance might make him complicit in the fraud."

"All the more reason not to raise the issue with him yet. The lawyers need to consider all this, and I need your prelim, James."

I spent the remainder of the morning and early afternoon dictating a preliminary report for Barry. Thankfully, the only interruption was from Simon just after I had handed the preliminary report to Mavis for finalising. He wanted a letter report checked, which was easy as it was well-written. I handed it back to him complimenting him on his brevity then checked my report which Mavis had formalised very efficiently.

Sometimes I rode my luck. I emailed my report to Barry, then almost immediately Sheena called. "I've been at a new scene today, James, an industrial unit in Staines, and I'd like you to investigate it. The fire was last night. Insurers weren't keen to appoint forensics as the fire brigade say that someone broke in and deliberately started the fire at nine o'clock last night, so on the face of it, there is no possibility of a repudiation against the insured. Unfortunately, the business wasn't doing well, and in view of what you did at Dagenham Glass last week, I persuaded insurers to appoint you."

"Thank you, what are the details?"

"The premises is occupied by a business engaged in the printing, storage and distribution of advertising literature. The unit is like the Dagenham Glass building with an office block and roller shutter access door at the front and printing and storage in the main part of the building at the rear, but it's not quite as high as the Dagenham Glass building and is only about half the plan area. The office block is only single story. Also, there was no high-rack storage. The advertising literature was stored in cardboard boxes on pallets, and the palletised stock was piled two high forming a large rectangular stack which was about a metre lower than the eaves. The fire brigade found a ladder at the rear extending up to the eaves. They think the arsonist climbed up the ladder and dropped onto the stack by breaking the nearest skylight to the eaves."

"How severe is the fire damage?"

"There is a lot of smoke damage, but the direct fire damage is not as severe as at Dagenham Glass. The arsonist started fires in the kitchen and amongst papers in two of the offices and also tried to ignite some of the cardboard boxes of stock on the pallets in the printing and storage area, but none of the fires really got going. There is still a substantial claim for smoke damage though. The printing machine, which was expensive, was positioned next to the stack and was severely soot damaged."

"How did the arsonist leave the building?"

"Through the printing and storage area rear fire exit door. The fire brigade found it open."

"The office doors weren't locked?"

"No, this is a family business, husband, wife, daughter and a friend of the husband who has worked there for years, so they never bothered about locking internal doors, but there were intruder alarm contacts on all the internal and external doors and PIRs throughout the building."

"What time did everyone leave?"

"The three family members, the Burtons, were going on holiday to Prague for a week, so they and the family friend, Paul Pike, departed at 1630 hours, setting the alarm and securing the unit as they left. The flight was at 1955 hours from Heathrow. The alarm company received an alarm signal at 2102 hours and called the Burtons, but upon receiving no answer, they called Mr Pike who was the other named person on their list. Mr Pike lives about ten-minute's drive from the premises. He arrived shortly after 2115 hours, and when he entered the reception to switch off the alarm, he smelt smoke so called the fire brigade."

"Any CCTV evidence?"

"No, but the intruder alarm control box was reasonably sophisticated, and I managed to access the log today with Mr Pike's assistance. I photographed each line of the log as we scrolled through it on the display, and I can send you my photographs, but it is as I said: the alarm was set at 1630 hours, and the next signal received by the alarm company's central station was the 2102-hours alarm signal, which was from a PIR movement detector in the printing and storage area, presumably activated by the intruder. There were then a series of alarm signals over the next few minutes from the office door contacts and the PIRs in the offices, again probably caused by the arsonist, with the final alarm signal being the contacts on the rear fire exit door at 2109 hours."

"So just over five minutes before Mr Pike arrived."

"Yes, and he arrived at the front and didn't see anybody."

"Presumably the family have been informed."

"They have, but they've decided to finish their holiday in Prague. Markham's been appointed, and he says that he can handle the claim whilst they're away as it's a straightforward case."

"How on earth was Markham appointed if the family were on a flight to Prague when the fire occurred?"

"He attended the scene shortly after the fire brigade and spoke to Mr Pike. Mr Pike in turn called the husband, Mr Mark Burton, when the family landed in Prague and explained what had happened. Markham was still at the scene and asked to speak to Mr Burton who then appointed Markham. Markham is fuming, by the way, that we're appointing you, given the circumstances, and he would like you to complete your inspection before the Burtons return from holiday."

"Depending on what I find at the scene, I might need to interview them."

"I've told Markham that might be necessary, and he started ranting and raving, so I didn't press the point; but let me know if you do need to speak to the Burtons."

"I can attend the scene tomorrow. How do I gain access?"

"Mr Pike has got keys for the premises, and he's expecting your call." Sheena gave me Mr Pike's telephone number.

"One other point about Markham," continued Sheena, "is that the lawyers appointed by the insurers of Dagenham Glass have advised there is a good case for repudiating liability, and the insurers have asked me to write a formal letter to Markham informing him that they will not be paying the claim. They are also considering sending your preliminary report to the police. I haven't written to Markham yet, and I'll wait until after you inspect the Burtons' premises because I suspect Markham will go into orbit when he receives the letter."

"Good idea. I don't think I'll be on Markham's Christmas card list. Sheena, I do have some concerns already on the Burtons' case. Firstly, if it was arson by someone who broke in, what was the motive? And are the police involved?"

"The police have attended, and I have spoken to the detective constable dealing with the case this afternoon. He said that the local area is blighted by a youth who is engaged in vandalising bus shelters, spraying graffiti and setting fire to public waste bins. He is from a problem family and the police think that he probably started the fire at the Burtons' unit."

"I'm astonished the police think that. From what you've described, the youth seems to be engaged in casual, opportunistic acts of relatively low-level damage, but this fire at the Burtons' unit sounds like it was planned and carried out by someone who was determined to cause damage to the business by bringing a ladder, forcing an entry and starting multiple fires throughout the premises. That, it seems to me, isn't the modus operandi of the youth who doesn't sound like has previously broken into a building."

"I am actually a little disturbed by the police linking the Burtons' fire to the youth and, of course, the business not doing well doesn't make me feel any easier, which is why I'm speaking to you."

"How did the arsonist get the ladder there and subsequently leave the area, given that Mr Pike didn't see anyone at the front when he arrived just after 2115 hours?"

"The unit is on a small industrial estate on the outskirts of Staines, and there is a narrow country lane and layby at the rear. The police wonder if the arsonist could have parked in the layby then lifted the ladder over the short fence between the layby and the narrow strip of wasteland at the rear of the Burtons' unit. Thereafter, the arsonist could have carried the ladder over to the building and placed it up against the rear wall."

"Presumably, the police are checking whether this youth can drive and whether he has access to a vehicle that can carry a ladder," I said dryly.

"I'll keep in contact with the police and let you know if I hear anything, James."

"Thanks, Sheena. It would be helpful, however, if I could just continue this discussion for a few minutes, particularly as the Burtons aren't going to be there when I attend tomorrow. One of my other immediate concerns is that this is still a reasonably high building, so if an intruder had broken a skylight without knowing what was below it, there would have been a risk of the intruder falling directly onto the floor beneath, which could have been fatal."

"Couldn't the arsonist have shone a torch in through the broken skylight to check what was inside?"

"How many skylights were broken?"

"Just one but that wasn't the only skylight above the stack."

"You can see my concern though that this apparently random arsonist, as well as taking a lot of time and trouble to start a number of fires, managed to choose a building with a stack of goods that conveniently extended close to the underside of some of the skylights. In relation to that, I am now wondering how the arsonist got down from the stack to start the fires."

"Well, at one end of the stack, some boxes of stock were arranged in a configuration like steps, extending from the floor to the top of the stack."

"The more I hear of this, the more I don't like it."

"As I've said, James, I'm also concerned, but one point in the Burtons' favour is that Mr Burton's pet parrot died in the fire, and Mr Pike said that Mr Burton had had it twenty-five years and loved it."

"What!" I gasped. "Tell me more, Sheena. I'm intrigued."

"Mr Burton kept a pet parrot, Joey, in his office, and it died during the fire, presumably from smoke inhalation."

"I thought I'd heard everything but evidently not. Was anyone looking after Joey whilst the Burtons were on holiday?"

"Mr Pike was going to be working in the unit every day to keep the business running whilst the Burtons were away, and he was going to feed and water Joey."

"A dead parrot sounds like a sentimental ploy to deflect people from asking penetrating questions."

"Fact is it is dead, James, and the police are convinced by it."

"From what you've told me previously about the police, I'm not surprised they are convinced. Also, it's convenient that the Burtons were at 30,000 feet when the fire occurred."

"Good luck, James. I'll send you the alarm log photographs."

"Before you go, I assume from our discussion that you are appointed by the insurers of the Burtons. Has anyone been appointed to investigate the fire for the insurers of the building?"

"The insurers of the Burtons' business coincidently also insure the owners of the building, so there is no point in instructing anyone else. The insurers have appointed me and will deal with any conflicts of interest between the Burtons and the owners of the building internally. The insurers are basically wondering whether they have a repudiation against the Burtons."

"So Willoughbys won't be involved on this one. Is Isaac appointed by Markham?"

"Not yet."

Shortly after we finished the call, Sheena emailed me her photographs of the alarm log. Given Sheena's description of the building, the log was as would have been expected if someone had forced an entry into the Burtons' unit's printing and storage area then had entered the kitchen and offices, returned to the printing and storage area and exited via the rear fire exit door. The first alarm sensor to activate was a PIR movement detector in the printing and storage area, after which the contacts on the kitchen door and on two of the office doors activated, consecutively followed by another activation of the same PIR movement detector in the printing and storage area, with the final activation been the contacts on the fire exit door.

I called Mr Pike. "Hello, Mr Pike, my name is James Gabriel from Jacobs, fire investigators, and I'm calling about the fire at the Burtons' unit."

"I don't care if you're the Archangel Gabriel, I'm not answering any of your questions, mate," said Mr Pike with a pronounced Cockney accent.

"I'm ringing to arrange access to the Burtons' unit. Can you meet me there at eight o'clock tomorrow morning and open up for me?"

"You can come to my house and collect the keys, mate, but

I'm not going to the unit with you as you'll start asking me questions."

I decided not to ask Mr Pike who had evidently given him instructions not to answer my questions. It had to be Markham.

"That's fine. What is your address?"

Mr Pike gave me his address in Staines, and we agreed that I would attend at his house at 0745 hours the next day.

Jemima was tired after an all-day meeting on a high-value case with an arrogant, patronising private client. I offered sympathy and understanding as I sometimes encountered similar loss adjusters, lawyers and insurers. Dealing with such people was problematic, but my previous advice to Jemima was to play the long game: let the immediate snide comments wash over you, and only change your views if you are satisfied with the logic of the arguments because, ultimately, it is those arguments that will prevail. The look on Jemima's face indicated she did not want a repeat of that advice. I held her close, ran my fingers through her hair and suggested she watched television whilst I cooked dinner.

She said, "No, I'd rather sit in the kitchen whilst you cook and tell me what happened with the summer jacket. It should take my mind off the day I've had."

She was right on that point. She was disturbed when I told her about the summer jacket and alarmed when I told her about the new Burtons' case and what Sheena had said on the Dagenham Glass case. She said, "Whatever the cause of the fire at Mr Gerash's property – and I am inclined to think bags of waste were deliberately piled up against the heater – you are correct that insurers can repudiate the entire claim if one part is found to be fraudulent. I think you've got enough evidence to show the summer jacket was burned and planted after the fire, so

I think the lawyers will advise insurers to repudiate the claim. The insurers on the Dagenham Glass case are also declining liability; it's near certain the insurers will refuse to pay up on Marty's mobile home fire; and I already think you will probably find some damning evidence on the Burtons' involvement in the fire at their unit. So Markham isn't going to be paid on at least three of those cases, possibly all four. Sheena is right, Markham will be bug-eyed when he hears about these repudiations, and he will blame you for most of them."

"He'll be all right about it. He's in the same golf club as Marty."

"It's not something to be funny about," Jemima snapped back with tension in her voice.

I turned off the hob ring I was working on, walked over to her and kissed her on the forehead. "I know. I'm sorry, I shouldn't have joked about it. I'm keeping a very watchful eye on Markham."

We ate my casserole in an uncomfortable, tired silence, but we both started to relax on the second glass of Pinot Grigio. Jemima initially didn't want to play Scrabble afterwards, but I persuaded her to play for half an hour and she relaxed some more. She then went to bed whilst I washed up. Thankfully, she was sleeping soundly when I joined her in bed.

Chapter 13

Dawn was just breaking and there was a heavy rainstorm when I parked in the drive of Mr Pike's semi-detached bungalow in Staines. There were no signs of life and no porch, which was unfortunate as I had not brought an umbrella and my raincoat did not have a hood. I stood outside the front door with my right-hand forefinger on the doorbell and my left hand holding my clipboard as a makeshift rain hood over my head.

After a few minutes, Mr Pike, flabby, bleary-eyed and wearing an untidy pullover and rumpled pyjama bottoms answered the door. "What the hell do you want?" he asked with an annoyed, raised voice.

"I'm James Gabriel from Jacobs. We spoke yesterday. I've come to collect the keys for the Burtons' unit."

"Oh, yeah," he replied, slightly sheepishly as his brain cells fired to one level above semi-conscious. "You better come in while I look for them," he continued, as he finally became aware of the rain sweeping into the hall.

I didn't like the implication that he was not confident he knew where the keys were and the related possibility that he would not find them.

"This fire business has muddled my routine, mate," he said by way of explanation, then continued, "just wait here while I find the keys."

Mr Pike walked along the hall into what looked like a kitchen at the rear, leaving me to contemplate the hall decor.

Everything had seen better days. The wallpaper and the carpets looked about twenty years old, and there was dust and grime on the two landscape pictures hanging on the hall wall. Mr Pike was in his late fifties, and I wondered if his other half had left him some years ago.

Any further, unkind thoughts about Mr Pike were suddenly ended by someone saying in an awkward, slightly raucous voice, "Harry Markham is a w…"

My jaw literally fell open. The voice appeared to come from the front-left room door which I was standing next to and which was slightly ajar. I then heard Mr Pike, evidently still in the kitchen, say, "Let me think, did I put them in this drawer?" The sound of a drawer opening then emanated from the kitchen, so I took the opportunity to push open the front-left room door.

As I did so, the awkward, slightly raucous voice said, "Who the hell are you?"

The source of the voice was a large parrot, perched in a cage which I thought was too small for it. The parrot made some more obscene remarks about Harry Markham and some complimentary comments on Mr Burton, all of which were interspersed by the sounds of cupboard doors being opened and closed in the kitchen and various frustrated outbursts from Mr Pike on his so far fruitless attempt to find the keys.

I pulled the door of the front-left room to its previous ajar position, and after a few minutes, Mr Pike walked triumphantly from the kitchen holding the keys in front of him. I was looking at one of the landscape pictures and simply said, "Great, thank you."

I was unsure as to whether he had heard the parrot as he made no comment on what it had said but he did glance at the front-left room door. The parrot itself made no further remark until I opened the front door and said to Mr Pike, "I'll drop the keys back later."

I faintly heard the parrot say, "Go to hell," as I walked out. Mr Pike immediately began coughing in an attempt, I thought, to disguise what the parrot had said. "Just put the keys through the letterbox," he said, then quickly closed the front door.

The rain stopped during the short drive to the Burtons' unit which was on a small industrial estate with four other similar units. I parked in front of the Burtons' unit, climbed out of my car, opened the boot and slipped on my overalls, noting that two of the other units were equipped with external CCTV cameras whilst, as Sheena had advised, the Burtons' unit had no CCTV cameras.

I decided firstly to speak to the occupiers of the units with the CCTV cameras. They both advised me that the police had taken their respective CCTV recordings for the evening of the fire but that the recordings simply showed Mr Pike attending shortly after 2115 hours and the fire brigade arriving ten minutes later. None of the CCTV cameras were directed at either the roof or the rear elevation of the Burtons' unit.

The theme of the day was evidently parrots. As I left the second unit, a flock of screeching ring-necked parakeets flew overhead.

I walked to the rear of the Burtons' unit where, by observation, I accepted that it was possible for someone to have parked in the layby, lifted a ladder over the short fence and carried the ladder to the rear of the unit. The layby was, however, on a secluded country road and there were no lights, so such ladder activities would not have been easy during a winter evening.

I returned to the front, unlocked the reception door and entered the Burtons' unit. A corridor provided access between the reception area and a kitchen, toilets and three offices in the single-storey, integral office block. Another door at the end of the corridor led to the printing and storage area.

The intruder alarm system was as described by Sheena. The fire alarm system comprised break glass cells.

Fires had been started in the kitchen, in two of the offices and in the printing and storage area. The plastic waste bin in the kitchen had been ignited, probably by the direct application of a lit match or lighter to waste packaging in the bin, and the ensuing fire had developed to destroy the chipboard work surface above the bin and the adjacent chipboard units. This fire had not, however, progressed to destroy all the kitchen units, probably due to the early intervention of the fire brigade.

The two offices where fires had occurred each contained a desk. In both offices, papers appeared to have been taken from the desktop and shelves, then piled under the desk and ignited. These fires were small and had not spread away from under the desks, most likely because the heat output from the ignited papers had been insufficient for initiating a sustained fire in the desk timbers – inadequate paper had been used. I suspected that these fires had almost self-extinguished before the fire brigade arrived. I noticed no smells of flammable liquid residues, such as petrol, amongst the debris or elsewhere in the offices and kitchen.

Papers had also been piled under the desk in the third office, but strangely, no attempt had been made to ignite those papers. Also, it was clear from an examination of the soot deposits on the doors and door frames that during the incident, the kitchen door and the doors of the two offices in which fires had occurred had been open. By way of comparison, the door of the third office –

in which the paper under the desk had not been ignited – had been closed.

The dead parrot was in a large cage in one of the offices in which a fire had burned under the desk. The parrot itself was smaller than the parrot at Mr Pike's house and had a relatively long tail, being about the same size and shape as a ring-necked parakeet. I photographed the bird then opened its cage and lifted it from the base. A clear, unsooted shape of the bird was revealed on the base, so the bird had evidently died before much soot had deposited during the fire. I photographed the shape.

The parrot itself was covered in soot, but in the light of my torch, its body colour seemed to be lime green – like a ring-necked parakeet. I took the bird into the toilets and partly rinsed the soot from the bird's neck. This revealed the body colour was indeed lime green and that there were black and red rings around the neck, which convinced me the bird was a ring-necked parakeet. I took the bird outside and placed it in a sample bag.

Five attempts had been made to start fires at the stack of goods in the printing and storage area. In each case, the plastic wrapping had been partly torn from a cardboard box of stock on a pallet and a naked flame had been applied to the surface of the exposed box. Unlike in the Dagenham Glass fire, however, the flame had not progressed into the box and had only spread upwards over the ignited cardboard box surface for a few centimetres from the point of ignition after which the flame had evidently self-extinguished.

In the Dagenham Glass case, the cardboard boxes had contained glassware and loose combustible packaging, an arrangement which meant the packaging was well aerated by the air spaces in the box and which resulted in the box and packaging burning readily when ignited and a continuing fire developed. By way of comparison, the Burtons' advertising literature almost completely filled each cardboard box and was in tight packs so was only exposed to the air externally. It followed that a small, initiating flame could not readily spread into a box, so there was almost no continuing flame at the box with the result that the upward spread of the flame was not supported and the flame extinguished.

With a little ingenuity, the arsonist might have started sustained fires at the Burtons' stack by, for example, forming piles of torn cardboard and paper on the floor next to the stack and igniting those piles in order to create a large initiating flame. My impression, however, was that with the alarm sounding and having apparently successfully started fires in the kitchen and in two of the offices, the arsonist was in panic mode upon returning to the printing and storage area. In my view, the arsonist had quickly torn plastic wrapping from some of the stock and had applied naked flames to the exposed cardboard boxes believing that those fires would immediately develop but had either not checked that those fires had progressed or seeing the flames self-extinguish, had simply moved to a new location to ignite another box. After five failed attempts, the arsonist had rushed to the fire exit door and departed.

The large printing-machine was very close to one end of the stack. It was severely soot damaged but had suffered no direct fire damage. Nonetheless, it was clear that if a fire had developed in the stack, the printing-machine would have been severely damaged.

I made my way to the end of the stack where some cardboard boxes of stock were arranged in a step configuration, and I climbed to the top of the stack. There were several sets of footprints in the soot on the steps and on top of the stack, presumably from the police and fire brigade personnel.

Unlike the Dagenham Glass skylights, the Burtons skylights were wired-glass constructions, and the entire pane of the forced skylight had fallen from its frame onto the stack. An impact crater, possibly caused by a hammer blow, was in the middle of the pane, and fractures radiated outwards from the crater, but the wire matrix had largely prevented the pane from separating into individual pieces. The police had presumably photographed the pane and had thought it unlikely that there were any fingerprints on it so had not retained it.

I took my own photographs, and as I did so, I noticed that there were some used cigarette ends on the plastic wrapping covering the top of the stack in the immediate area around the forced skylight pane. I counted ten cigarette ends, most of which were difficult to see because they had fallen into various crevices and hollows created in the plastic wrapping by the people who had walked on the stack. Also, a few of the cigarette ends had been squashed, presumably because someone had stood on them.

I had inspected previous fire incidents where investigators who had attended before me had smoked and discarded cigarette ends at the scene, but I had only found one or two cigarettes on those occasions. I picked up one of the un-squashed cigarette ends from a crevice and observed that it was a common brand. I also noticed that there were a lot of soot particles on the cigarette end, and I presumed these had adhered to the cigarette end when it had rolled over the plastic wrapping into the crevice after the fire. I checked the other un-squashed cigarette ends and observed that these were also sooted.

I then chided myself for presuming a pat answer for the cigarette ends and the soot on them. Was it really plausible that so many cigarettes were smoked and discarded by investigators in one small area of a scene, bearing in mind that it takes about ten to twenty minutes to smoke a cigarette? I thought of another disturbing explanation for the cigarette ends, which also accounted for some other issues with the case and which prompted me to lift up one side of the forced skylight pane.

I observed that there was no soot on the plastic sheeting underneath the pane, so evidently, I had found the pane in the position it was occupying at the time of the fire: neither the fire brigade nor the police had moved it. I also observed that there were two used cigarette ends under the pane and that there was no soot on those cigarette ends. I photographed those cigarette ends in position then retained them and placed them in small sample bags.

I next looked again at the fractured skylight pane. The impact crater was on the surface facing upwards and there was no sealing mastic on the edges of that upper surface. The latter point puzzled me because an examination of the skylight frame, which was still in situ in the roof opening, revealed that the only remains of sealing mastic were on the upper part of the frame. There should have been corresponding remains of mastic left on the edges of the upper surface of the pane when it was forced from the frame, but the only mastic was on the edges of the lower surface of the pane – and there was no mastic on the corresponding lower edge of the frame.

I deduced that the pane had flipped over when it had fallen with the result that it had landed on its exterior surface, originally the upper surface but now the lower surface. It followed that the impact crater was on the internal surface of the pane, now the upper surface. It further followed that the skylight pane had been forced out of the frame by an impact applied to its internal surface from inside the unit and that the pane had fallen back into the unit, flipping over as it fell.

I decided to retain the forced skylight pane and the sooted cigarette ends and spent some time taking photographs, drawing a plan of the top of the stack and making measurements to show the positions of the pane and cigarette ends, after which I placed the items in sample bags. As always, I also drew plans of the unit and took photographs showing the separate areas of fire damage and the soot damage throughout the building. Finally, I photographed the ladder, which had been brought into the unit and was lying on the floor against the rear wall of the unit. I wondered if it had been there before the incident.

When I put the keys through Mr Pike's letterbox, I placed my ear against the opening and smiled because I heard the parrot repeating some of its sayings on Markham.

It was only midday, so I decided to drive into the office. I wanted, in particular, to deliver the broken skylight and the dead parakeet to the office basement sample store in order to save me driving in through the rush-hour traffic on the following morning. I parked in the small, public car park next to the office an hour later, a little tired from the scene work, but the drive was straightforward, and I had crystallised a lot of thoughts during the journey. I took the samples into the basement then went to see Jane Gainor. She was beaming.

"Hello, James, I won the court case."

"Brilliant, well done! I thought you would. What did the judge say?"

"He said I gave my evidence with confidence and authority and he had no hesitation in accepting my opinion. Mind you, he also said the other side's retired plumber lacked sufficient metallurgical knowledge."

"That doesn't actually have a bearing on your evidence. I know of cases where the judge didn't like any of the side's experts and criticised them all. It's a well-earned victory at the start of your career."

"Thank you."

"I've got two queries on one of my cases, one straightforward, the other a little unusual."

"Go on," said Jane, raising her eyebrows questioningly.

"It's a deliberate fire in an industrial unit with a forced skylight, and I would like to know from which side the skylight was forced. I think I know but I would like your view."

"And the 'little unusual' query?"

"There was a dead parakeet in a cage in one of the offices, and I would like you to X-ray the parakeet."

"I hope you're not expecting me to revive the parakeet, James," said Jane, slightly wide-eyed.

I grinned. "I think the owner of the unit arranged for the fire to be deliberately started. He was reportedly a parrot lover, in which case, I don't think he'd have wanted the parakeet to have suffered during the fire. I wonder if he broke its neck before the fire."

"Okay, James, I'll have a look at them for you. I'm sure our X-ray machine can handle a dead parakeet. You never know what is going to happen next at Jacobs!"

"Thanks! The samples are labelled on my shelves in the basement store."

I decided not to call Sheena with my preliminary conclusions. Rather, I spent the remainder of the afternoon dictating a draft preliminary letter report, which helped me to refine my thoughts. I decided to postpone sending it until the next day. I left the office shortly after five p.m. and drove home.

Chapter 14

Jemima said, "So you think the Burtons left someone inside the unit when they departed on the evening of the fire; and before the alarm was set, that someone, the arsonist, climbed up one end of the stack which had been deliberately arranged in a step configuration, then spent the evening sitting under a skylight close to the eaves, a position that was out of range of the movement detectors?"

"Yes."

"The arsonist was occupied during that time smoking cigarettes?"

"Yes, again, but the arsonist probably also passed the time watching videos or playing games on a mobile telephone."

"And shortly before nine p.m., the arsonist reached up and broke the skylight, possibly with a hammer, and the skylight fell inside, flipping over and landing on top of two of the discarded cigarette ends?"

"Another yes. When the fires subsequently occurred, those two cigarette ends were protected by the skylight from the soot, but the other cigarette ends, unprotected on top of the stack, became covered in soot."

"At about nine p.m., the arsonist climbed down the stack setting off a PIR movement detector in the printing and storage area then went into the kitchen and two of the offices and started fires?"

"You are too good at this."

"Why didn't the arsonist start a fire in the third office, having gone to all the trouble of piling up paper under the desk?"

"I don't think the arsonist went into the third office after starting the fires in the other two offices. I've checked the alarm evidence, and it shows that the third office door wasn't opened until after the fire brigade attended, so it must have been opened by the fire brigade. I think the papers were piled under the desks before the Burtons and Mr Pike left, then the office doors were closed in order to allow the alarm to be set as there were contacts on the doors. All the arsonist had to do was go into the kitchen and offices and apply naked flames to the waste materials in the kitchen waste bin and to the papers under the office desks, but the arsonist panicked after setting the fire in the second office so missed out the third office and went straight to the printing and storage area to start the fires there."

"Why were piles of paper not placed next to the stack to allow fires to become established there?"

"I suspect the Burtons and the arsonist never thought it would be necessary. They probably thought that applying a naked flame to the cardboard boxes of stock forming the stack would result in fires taking off immediately and quickly, but they were wrong – and a little unlucky."

"I think you're probably right, but why do it that way? Why not arrange for the arsonist to break in through the skylight?"

"Because that is a lot more difficult and riskier. The arsonist would have to climb up a high ladder in the dark, which risks falling and would probably have to use a torch, which risks discovery, even though there was only a quiet country road at the rear. Also, the arsonist would then have to break the skylight and climb in which again risks a fall. It would be less risky both from the safety and discovery perspective for the arsonist to be left in the building on top of the stack. The ladder might even have been placed up against the rear of the building just before everyone left at 1630 hours, when it was dusk, to save the arsonist from having to do it later. They could have measured the internal distance between the fire exit door and the skylight that was going to be forced, then measured the same distance externally so they would know where the ladder needed to be positioned. Thereafter, in the dark, with no one attempting to do anything externally with a torch, there was almost no chance that the ladder would be discovered until the fire brigade arrived."

"If the arsonist's car had been left in the layby for a quick getaway after leaving via the fire exit door, there was still a risk, albeit small, that the police would drive down the country road before the fire and wonder why a car was parked there on a winter's night with no sign of the owner."

"If I am right, the ladder might have been brought to the unit and left inside during the days or weeks before the fire in which case, there would have been no need for a car or other vehicle to be parked in the layby on the evening of the fire. The arsonist could have run out the fire exit door, climbed over the fence and walked along the country road until reaching the main road into Staines where the arsonist might either live or have parked a car. Alternatively, Mr Pike could have picked up the arsonist on the way to the unit after being called by the alarm company. Mr Pike could have driven along the country road to the layby, and the arsonist could have got into his car and lain on the rear seat whilst Mr Pike drove to the front of the unit."

"So, Mr Pike must have been part of the plot? He doesn't seem that bright, forgetting you were going to call at his home to collect the keys then forgetting where the keys were."

"I think he's a bit lazy, which was compounded by him just

145

having woken up when I called, but he's tough: he refused to answer my questions or come to the scene with me. I think he must be part of the plot. Sheena was told by either Markham or Mr Pike himself that everyone left together at 1630 hours, and that timing is supported by the alarm timings. If Mr Pike did leave with everyone else at 1630 hours, then he must be part of the plot because he would have known that the arsonist was left in the unit on top of the stack, that piles of paper had been placed under the office desks and, if I'm right, that the ladder had been positioned up against the rear of the building. If he didn't leave at 1630 hours, if for example he left earlier, then he still must be part of the plot because for some reason he has lied in saying he left at 1630 hours. I think though that he is deeply involved in the plot."

"You think he's the arsonist?"

"No, he can't be because the alarm company called him, and I'll check but I think alarm companies always demand that they are provided with landline numbers for their contacts list, so Mr Pike must have been at home when the alarm company called him, which was shortly after the alarm activated. I might never identify the arsonist, but the police might if they ever become properly interested in the case."

"What do you think Mr Pike's role was?"

"To attend the unit, discover the fire and call the fire brigade – and as I've just said, probably to pick up the arsonist on the way to the unit – then to be the point of contact whilst the Burtons were on their alibi holiday; and also, to look after Mr Burton's parrot which had been swapped for a dead parakeet."

"You don't know that."

"We'll see what the X-ray results show, but those notwithstanding, I don't think the parrot-loving Mr Burton would have left Joey to die in the fire. I think Joey was in Mr Pike's bungalow, bearing in mind also that the parrot's sayings were complimentary to the Burtons and disparaging about Markham."

"That latter point raises a whole lot of other issues."

"It certainly does. I attended Mr Pike's bungalow less than a day and a half after the fire, and I think Mr Pike spent most of his waking hours during that time dealing with the fallout from the fire. I don't think he had time to say derogatory remarks about Markham to Joey, and I think also that Joey might need to hear such remarks for quite a few days or weeks and possibly months before he repeats them. I think Harry Markham has known Mark Burton for a long time, long enough anyway for Mr Burton to have doubts about some aspects of Markham's character and to have taught Joey to say what he said today.

"I think Markham knew the Burtons' business was in financial difficulties and that he offered them a way out. He conspired with them to start these fires in the unit such that it would appear the arsonist was an intruder who had forced an entry. Markham offered to deal with the claim with some assistance from Mr Pike whilst the Burtons were on holiday. As I've previously told you, I think also that Markham conspired with the insureds to deliberately start the fires at Dagenham Glass, Marty's mobile home and the Mr Gerash property."

Jemima said, "And you think he did that in part because the loss assessing world is very competitive so he wanted to make sure those cases were his before the fires occurred?"

"Yes, but I also suspect it was Markham who initiated the idea of starting the fires when he found out through various friends of friends and contacts that the businesses or individuals were in difficulty and/or, as in the mobile home case, the insured was probably amenable to making some money by fraud. I saw

Markham at Ascot with Ronnie Stanshaw and the insured from Marty's mobile home fire – I checked Marty's scene photographs and one of Markham's Ascot companions was clearly in the background of one of them. It would be very unusual for a loss assessor to attend a race meeting with an insured a few days after a major fire, and Markham attended with two insureds – possibly a third, I haven't checked yet – and the only plausible explanation in my view is that he knew them well. I've got timed and dated photographs showing them together at Ascot looking very matey.

"I was always concerned as to how he managed to get the Dagenham Glass case. He couldn't have got to the scene until about ten o'clock at night, by which time, it was highly likely that other loss assessors would have attended and offered their services. Markham would have liked to have been there to be in control of the situation, which is why he asked the judge in Jane's case if he could give his evidence early. He wasn't going to a golf club dinner that evening or to any assignation. He wanted to get back to Dagenham so he could arrive just after the fire but he didn't need to be there as he'd already arranged it with Ronnie Stanshaw.

"He probably called Ronnie Stanshaw from the court at lunchtime to let him know the situation and again – when Jane saw him – after he left court late in the afternoon to tell Ronnie Stanshaw he wouldn't get there until ten p.m. but to go ahead with the fire and fend off any other loss assessors who attended by saying he, Markham, had called him shortly after the fire, had sold his services to him and was now handling the claim for Dagenham Glass. The other loss assessors would have thought Markham had been called by a fire brigade contact – like them – and would have had no choice anyway but to accept Mr Stanshaw's decision.

"As to Marty's mobile home fire, Markham attended the scene very shortly after the fire and told the loss adjuster, Barry, that he had been at another scene in Kent that day. On the same day, however, he told our associate, Simon, that he'd only attended one other case in Kent this year, and we know that was the Mr Gerash case. Markham dropped his guard there, but he probably didn't think anyone would start questioning how he'd got to the mobile home shortly after the fire because that is what loss assessors do.

"As a matter of logic, Markham's statements to Barry and Simon could be reconciled if he had visited the Mr Gerash property on the day he attended Marty's mobile home fire. I think, however, it is unlikely that Markham would say to Barry, who was dealing with the Mr Gerash case, that he had been to another scene in Kent that day if he had actually been to the Mr Gerash property, although I accept that Markham might have been trying to mislead Barry. But I just don't buy the explanation that Markham had gone all the way to Kent to check the Mr Gerash property because he'd heard we were probably going to be instructed. That's tripe. I don't think he was at any other property that day. I think he'd gone down to Maidstone because he'd arranged with the insured of the mobile home for the fire to be started on that day and he made sure he was there with the insured just after the fire brigade attended."

Jemima said, "I think you'll struggle to show that Markham conspired with the insured on the Dagenham Glass and mobile home fires. The evidence on both is essentially circumstantial, even with the Ascot photograph, and I don't think the Crown Prosecution Service would run them. The Burtons' case conspiracy relies on what you heard a parrot say in an employee's home. You can't prove that the parakeet was swapped for that parrot even if the parakeet's neck was broken. Won't they just say its neck broke when it fell off its perch during the fire? Also, how did they catch the parakeet?"

"I don't know how they caught the parakeet although they might have bought one; it's probably not that important. But if the police were to take a real interest in the case, they could seize the parrot from Mr Pike's home and ask Mr Pike for an explanation as to why it is making remarks about Markham, a loss assessor who normally you would not have expected either Mr Pike or the Burtons to have known before the fire."

"Neither Mr Burton nor Mr Pike were in the Ascot photograph?"

"Mr Pike wasn't and I don't think Mr Burton was there."

"What I do think, James, is that there is enough evidence to show that all four incidents were fraudulent acts by the insureds, in which case, Markham won't be paid on any of them. Also, despite what I've said about proof, I think he did conspire with all those insureds, which means he is prepared to engage in serious criminal activity, and that heightens my concern as to what he might try to do to you, James."

"I'm on my guard, darling, and the best way to deal with Markham is to get the police interested in him. That might prove difficult because there are different insurers in each case and, as you've said, on an individual case basis the evidence against Markham is weak – although the four cases together might be enough to persuade the police to investigate Markham. Each insurer will probably repudiate liability and may well be prepared to advise the police of their individual insured's fraudulent behaviour. The insurers of the Burtons might also be willing to advise the police of my concerns on Markham depending on how the parrot evidence pans out, but the best evidence on Markham on two of the other cases, possibly the third, is my Ascot photograph, which might not be enough if each case is treated separately."

"One loss adjuster, Sheena, is dealing with the Dagenham Glass case and the Burtons' case and another loss adjuster, Barry, is dealing with the Mr Gerash and the mobile home fire, isn't that right?"

"Yes, and Barry is also dealing with the Dagenham Glass case for the insurers of the building owner who is not engaged in fraudulent activity, but Barry is certainly aware of my views on the cause of that fire and knows Markham is involved. If you're suggesting that Sheena and Barry together might be the way into Markham, I think you could be right."

"Just a thought," said Jemima.

"How was your day?"

"Lengthy discussions with that odious client and one of our partners but the client's increasingly long silences towards the end of the day indicated that he is accepting my arguments."

"Tell me the detail."

"No, I need to take my mind off it."

"Play a game?"

"I'm almost too tired but I'm going to force myself otherwise I won't sleep. Scrabble, please."

Scrabble it was, after which we were almost too tired to get ready for bed and certainly too tired for engaging in any other bedtime activity. We wrapped ourselves together and fell asleep easily, deeply and satisfyingly, knowing each other was there.

Chapter 15

The following morning, Friday, I arrived at the office at eight o'clock with the intention of checking my draft preliminary report on the Burtons' case so as to collect my thoughts before calling Sheena. As I arrived, I received a text from Jane, which stated:

"James, I have examined the skylight pane and x-rayed the parakeet. Very interesting results, especially the parakeet. I am in the office today if you want to discuss, but please see me early as I have visitors at 10.00."

I went straight to her office.

"Hi, James. I stayed on yesterday evening to deal with your exhibits as my visitors on one of my cases will be here most of the day."

"Thank you, Jane."

"The skylight pane first. There was an implication that you thought it had been forced from the inside, and you are correct, assuming the sealant is on the external edge of the pane, which I think it must be."

"Yes, to the sealant and to the implication."

Jane smiled. "And I think it was probably a blow from a hammer."

"Jolly good… and the parakeet?"

"It was shot."

"What!"

"There's an air-pellet-sized hole in its skull and an air pellet lodged in the brain. Oh, and its neck isn't broken."

"Well, well, that explains a few things. Also, the insured can't like parakeets that much if he was prepared to shoot it."

"Parakeets screech don't they? Perhaps he doesn't like them because of the noise they make but he likes other parrots."

"There was a noisy flock of them flying overhead when I was there. I wonder if at some time before the fire, the insured or an accomplice went out the back of the unit where it's fairly quiet, waited for a flock of parakeets and shot one with an air rifle. Anyway, thanks ever so much, Jane; that is very helpful."

"No problem, James."

In view of Jane's results, I made some changes to my draft report then I called Barry.

"Hello, James, insurers were very impressed with the ski jacket label evidence on the Mr Gerash case. They really want to repudiate liability on the case and are just waiting for the lawyers' advice on your preliminary report before pressing the button on a letter to Markham. Georgie was pleased as well. She thought she was going to be criticised for not excavating the clothing on the bed, but we now know that the summer jacket – and probably a lot more items – were planted after Georgie's scene inspection."

"Pleased to hear it on insurers and on Georgie… Barry, I saw Markham at Ascot races last week with three insureds. One was Ronnie Stanshaw, one was the insured on the mobile home fire that Marty is doing for you, and I suspect the other was Mr Gerash. If I email you a photograph, can you confirm whether it was Mr Gerash?"

"Of course," replied Barry slowly. "What's going on? Why were they all at Ascot together?"

"Let me send the photograph then I'll explain," I replied, as

I emailed the photograph.

After a short pause, whilst he opened the email, Barry said, "Yes, that's Mr Gerash with the others, as you've said."

"They were at Ascot races on the day after Marty attended his mobile home fire, which was the same week of the Dagenham Glass fire."

"That's very odd," said Barry with a deeply disturbed tone in his voice, "a loss assessor attends a major sporting event with three insureds, two of whom he only met that week when they suffered major fires and would be expected to be under some considerable stress and probably not inclined to be in a celebratory or gambling mood."

"I don't think Markham first met them that week."

"Go on."

"I don't know about Mr Gerash, but I think Markham has known Ronnie Stanshaw and the insured on Marty's case for some time, and I think he conspired with them to start their respective fires."

"Bloody hell!"

I told Barry the circumstantial evidence concerning Markham's involvement in the Dagenham Glass fire and Marty's fire. I could almost hear him wrinkle his nose. "I appreciate the evidence might seem weak," I continued, "particularly for a criminal court, although I would add that I've done another one yesterday for Sheena where there is some strong evidence that Markham conspired with the insured to deliberately start the fire." I decided not to provide Barry with the details of the parakeet and parrot evidence.

"Obviously, that's for Sheena to deal with," said Barry, retreating further from agreeing with me on Markham's involvement.

"Of course, and I'll be speaking with Sheena about that case after our conversation, but I think there are wider implications which could have very serious future consequences. If I'm right – and I think I am, otherwise, I wouldn't be speaking with you – Markham will continue with his serious fraudulent activities and insurers will have to pick up the bills. At some stage, Markham will be stopped, but I think we should at least alert insurers and the police now. Clearly, it's up to them how they proceed, but the insurers could ask loss adjusters to take a close look at all their current cases involving Markham and, in particular, future cases where he is involved. The police could carry out all sorts of investigations such as looking at telephone calls, texts and emails to establish any other evidence of links between Markham and the insureds before the fires."

"I did raise an eyebrow on the Mr Gerash case," said Barry, slightly uncomfortably. "When I was at the scene on the day after the fire, the fire brigade re-attended to check the fire was completely out, and the fire officer said that the first appliance to attend on the previous evening had reported a loss assessor 'who looked like Boycie from *Only Fools and Horses*' was already there with the insured. I wondered how Markham had managed to get there so quickly given he is based in North London, but I thought he must have been at another case in Kent that day, although it was a bit odd him still being in the area at eight o'clock in the evening when the fire occurred."

"Markham told one of the Jacobs associates that he has only done the Mr Gerash case and Marty's mobile home fire in Kent this year so he couldn't have been at another case in Kent on the day of the Mr Gerash fire."

Barry groaned. "How do you think we should proceed?" he asked.

"You are aware of three of the cases, even though your insured on the Dagenham Glass case wasn't fraudulent, and Sheena is involved in two of the cases, including the one this week that you're not involved in; so all four cases are covered by you and Sheena. Let me speak to Sheena. If she is in agreement, your good self and Sheena could ask all the insurers if they would agree to me referring to their respective cases in a draft statement that I could prepare for the police in which I could describe my concerns about Markham conspiring with the insureds to commit fraud. I would include what you have just told me on the Mr Gerash case. It would of course involve each insurer knowing about the other insurers' cases, but unless the insurers work together on this, Markham will be difficult to stop. Also, I think the statement would carry more weight if it was presented to the police by either you or Sheena or even better, jointly by the insurers themselves."

Barry was silent, a thoughtful pause, I hoped. "Okay, James, that sounds sensible. You speak to Sheena then ask her to call me. We can only put what you've got in front of the insurers and the police, and it's up to them as to how they proceed."

Sheena was appalled at my findings on the Burtons' case and shocked at my views on Markham's involvement.

"I had to nearly put a gun to insurers' head to appoint you on Burtons, James. Insurers just wanted to pay up as soon as the fire brigade said it was a break-in. The police didn't help mind, saying it was probably a local hooligan."

"Do you think the insurers will help with respect to Markham?"

"They might. From what you've said, it's near certain that they'll repudiate liability on the Burtons' case. Markham is more of a problem, but I'll warn insurers that if something is not done,

Markham will probably continue with his activities, which could affect the entire insurance industry. This is just the sort of issue that occurs in many industries and in public services where people are given a warning of illegal activity and have the opportunity to deal with it but sadly often don't because they can't be bothered to make the effort or hope it won't happen to them again. I'm with you on this one."

"Thank you, Sheena. Are you going to be taking statements from the Burtons and Mr Pike?"

"Almost certainly, but I'll have to wait until the Burtons return from holiday next week. I'd like you to send me your preliminary report with your conclusions on what you've found to date. Insurers will probably reserve their position and ask me to take statements that deal with the business finances and the various factual points in your report such as the configuration of the stack, the alarm specification and the security of the building. Markham will moan like mad but that's his problem. I think insurers will repudiate liability after the statements have been signed."

"Having regard to Markham, it would be worth asking the Burtons and Mr Pike whether they knew Markham before the fire."

"Because of the parrot evidence."

"Yes, the shot parakeet complements the skylight pane evidence that the arson was an inside job and indicates that the original parrot was moved from the Burtons' unit before the fire. The parrot at Mr Pike's home mentioned Harry Markham, which wouldn't have been possible unless either Mr Pike – and we will say also the Burtons, as the parrot was most likely the original parrot in the Burtons' unit – were very well acquainted with Markham before the fire. If Mr Burton, Mr Pike and Markham admit they already knew each other before the fire – as we say they did – that would immediately cast suspicion on Markham's involvement, so we think they will say that Markham was only introduced to the other two on the evening of the fire, Mr Pike in person and Mr Burton by telephone."

"And you will sign a statement saying that the parrot was saying Harry Markham's name only a day and a half after the fire so the implication is that they had all known each other for a long time and they are lying."

"Yes."

"Got it. I don't know if this will all hang together against Markham, but as we've discussed, I think we have to do it."

I provided Sheena with some more incriminating information concerning what the parrot had said and also told her what Barry had said, which I thought could nail Markham.

"Wow, James, I'll definitely ask the Burtons and Mr Pike whether they knew Markham before the fire, and I'll call Barry now."

"Thanks, Sheena, the prelim will be with you today."

After we finished the call, I checked my preliminary report again then emailed it to Sheena. I next decided to go to see Marty, and as I walked along the corridor leading to his office, Selena came out of the office and slightly composed herself when she saw me. She walked past me with only a slight colouring of her cheeks.

"Good morning, James."

"Good morning, Selena."

I wondered whether Marty and Selena now kept a close eye on the call indicator lights on Marty's office telephone when they were in his office together and in particular on my call indicator light so that Selena could leave shortly after I finished a call –

and before I could reach his office. That view was reinforced when I entered Marty's office and he slightly froze.

"Morning, James," said Marty, nervously clearing his throat.

"Morning, Marty. I don't think Markham was at another case on the day of your mobile home fire. I think he knew that fire was going to occur because he conspired with the insured to defraud the insurance company, and I think he has conspired with three other insureds to start fires for defrauding other insurers."

Marty relaxed slightly, I presumed because Selena wasn't on my agenda. "Crikey, don't beat about the bush, James!"

I told Marty of my evidence concerning Markham.

"I can see the problems with the evidence. It's largely circumstantial. The parrot evidence could be very good, but even if it's not, it's entertaining," said Marty.

"Taking it all together though, there is enough to warrant a police investigation."

"I think that's right, but as you've said, it would be better if they were approached by either the loss adjusters or the insurers together. It's a good job Sheena and Barry are involved. They're probably the best in the business."

"I think so too. I'm counting on them to persuade the insurers that they should go to the police."

"Thanks for letting me know."

"I thought you should be first to know, just in case he's blackballed at the golf club."

Marty chuckled. "There are already some raised eyebrows at the golf club. The story is that Markham became a loss assessor after leaving his previous job, the insurance brokers, under a cloud. Apparently, insurers had issued a policy to a new client on Markham's recommendation, only for the client to make a large claim for a fire within a month of the policy incepting. The insurers blamed Markham for not checking all the risks, and the broker asked him to leave."

"He might have been unlucky. Fires can occur anywhere at any time, even at those clients who follow good risk management procedures. Mind you, given what has happened, I wonder whether Markham set that one up for the insured. He could have obtained the policy for the client knowing there was going to be a fire. He would have earned a commission from the insurer for selling the policy and earned a backhand from the insured when the claim was paid. Alternatively, I wonder if it was being fired that prompted him to become a loss assessor, as some sort of act of revenge on insurers, with the shift to conspiring to start fires occurring when he realised how tough the loss assessing world was."

"You should put all that in your statement for the police. They might investigate Markham's previous life."

Chapter 16

A week later, Sheena called me.

"Hello, James, I interviewed Mark Burton and Mr Pike yesterday. Harry Markham was there, as he was entitled to be as he is representing them. He was quite aggressive, demanding to know why I wanted signed statements on a fire which the police and fire brigade agree was caused by an intruder. I simply said that insurers had requested statements, so I was following instructions.

"The atmosphere in the room went icy cold when I asked Mr Burton and Mr Pike whether they had known Markham before the fire. Markham said that was a disgraceful question and wanted to know what was going on. I said again that insurers had asked me to ask the question, and I refused to say why because, I said, I didn't want to lead Mr Burton's and Mr Pike's answers. Markham then said he hadn't known them before the fire, which of course immediately led Mr Burton and Mr Pike who both said, somewhat uneasily I thought, that they hadn't known Markham prior to the evening of the fire.

"I told them that the parakeet had been shot, and that was the first time during the interview that they all looked worried. Markham was quick-witted. He said the intruder had probably shot the parakeet. I told them you had found evidence that the skylight pane had been broken from the inside and that your view was that someone had been left in the unit. They denied that anyone had been left inside and said that your interpretation of the broken skylight pane was wrong. I told them also that your view was that the original bird in the cage had been removed before the fire and that the parakeet had been shot as a replacement, but I didn't tell them you had seen or heard the parrot at Mr Pike's home."

"Or what the parrot said about Markham?"

"Certainly not. Markham said you had got everything wrong, and in view of the issues that were raised in the interviews, he was advising Mr Burton and Mr Pike not to sign their statements until he obtained legal advice for them."

"He's deluded if he thinks a court will believe an intruder would have shot the parakeet, even in the unlikely event that an intruder would turn up with an air rifle."

"He said the intruder could have taken an air rifle to the Burtons' unit to defend himself then shot the parakeet out of compassion before starting the fire."

"If he wins that argument, we all might as well give up."

Within two weeks, all the insurers repudiated liability respectively on the Dagenham Glass, Mr Gerash, Marty's mobile home and Burtons' fires. Sheena and Barry had sent separate letters on each case to Markham stating that insurers would not be paying the claims, and the feedback I received from Sheena and Barry was that Markham was incandescent with rage. He told Sheena and Barry that all the clients would be suing their insurers. Sheena and Barry essentially advised Markham that we all looked forward to seeing him and the insureds in court.

I had also written and signed a statement describing my concerns about Markham's involvement in the four cases. All the insurers had agreed that the statement could be sent to the police, so Sheena had sent the document to the police officer dealing with the Burtons' fire. Subsequently, a detective chief inspector had requested copies of my preliminary reports on all four cases, which I provided with the insurers' consent.

It was now the third Friday in December, just over four weeks after my Burtons' inspection. Ascot racecourse was holding its Christmas race meeting today and tomorrow. I was working in the office today but was going to Ascot on Saturday.

Sheena called me just after lunch. "The police called me this morning, James. They arrested Harry Markham on Wednesday on suspicion of conspiring to defraud the insurers on the Dagenham Glass and Burtons' fires. They don't think there is enough evidence at the moment of his prior involvement on the mobile home and Mr Gerash fires despite the evidence of Barry and your associate Simon and your Ascot photograph, but they are still working on emails and text messages.

"Apparently, Markham was very careful at covering his tracks. The only incriminating calls the police have positively identified are two he made from Truro to Ronnie Stanshaw at about 12:30 p.m. and 4:15 p.m. on the day of the Dagenham Glass fire. Both calls were, of course, before the fire. Apparently, Markham is now claiming he did know Ronnie Stanshaw very well before the fire and that it was just a coincidence that he called him on the day the fire occurred. The police pointed out to Markham that if he knew Ronnie Stanshaw so well, it is surprising that these are the only two calls that they have found he ever made to him.

"The police strongly suspect that Markham has a false identity and that he used another mobile phone in the name of that false identity to set up the fires with Mr Stanshaw and the other insureds. He probably didn't have that mobile phone with him when he was in Truro because he thought the Dagenham Glass fire was all set up. Unfortunately for him, he was delayed giving evidence, so he used his legitimate mobile phone to call Mr Stanshaw at lunchtime, presumably to say he wouldn't arrive shortly after the fire, and again after he left court, which was observed by your associate, Jane, to let him know he was leaving Truro. He took a slight risk, but he didn't think someone like you would start wondering how he managed to sell his services to the Stanshaws."

"What about the parrot?"

"Well, regardless of the evidence on Markham's involvement, the police have separately arrested all the insureds on the four cases on suspicion of attempting to defraud the insurance companies. All the insureds have denied the charges. The police have leaned on them to cooperate with respect to Markham's involvement on the basis that if they do, their sentences will be reduced, but so far, none of them is admitting to fraud or to Markham conspiring with them. The parrot evidence may well undo Markham though the police attended Mr Burton's and Mr Pike's homes and found no parrots. There was, however, an empty cage at Mr Pike's home, and Mr Pike said that when you attended, he did have a parrot in the cage. Mr Pike said that the parrot subsequently died and that you are mistaken that it mentioned Harry Markham's name whilst you were there."

"I wonder whether Mr Pike first suspected I had heard the parrot mention Markham when you interviewed him and Mr Burton and asked them if they had known Markham before the fire? After the interview, they must have all discussed why you had asked them about Markham's involvement, and given the pressure they were all under, Mr Pike may have said that I might have heard the parrot say Markham's name. Mr Burton and

Markham must have been furious that Mr Pike had let me into his home, and Markham may have been livid that the parrot had been taught to say his name, but once they all calmed down, I think they must have realised the parrot had to go one way or another. It might not actually be dead, but it is undoubtedly in a place that the police will have difficulty finding."

"Anyway, the police think they have got enough evidence on the insureds and on Markham. No one has been charged yet, but the police are planning to send their files to the Crown Prosecution Service. Also, they are planning to speak to Isaac on the wording in his Mr Gerash report, the wording that you referred to in your statement. They are considering charging him with conspiring to defraud the insurer."

"Good, but I suspect he will claim bad draughtsmanship, and if you've read any of his other reports, you will probably agree he's got a point. Thanks for the update, anyway, Sheena. I'll watch my back if Markham is around."

Chapter 17

Samantha and Julie were in top form as they made my bacon butties.

"We've both got boyfriends, James, so you will be taking us to the races then?" said Samantha, winking at Julie.

"Two handsome hunks, I assume?"

"Of course, but you can judge for yourself when you meet them," said Julie, winking at Samantha.

"I look forward to it. Let me know some dates when you're free, and I'll take you. Tips, guided tour and introductions to the best bookmakers included."

"Really, you would take us?" asked Samantha, slightly incredulously.

"I said I would, and I'd like to. Dates, please!"

"Oh, thank you, James. So, we'll meet your wife?" asked Julie.

"You might but she probably won't come. She likes to do her own thing on Saturdays, although she might come to meet you and form a view on your boyfriends. She won't mind me taking you and your boyfriends to the races, even if she declined the invitation."

"You're lucky to have a wife like that, James," said Samantha.

"I know."

We exchanged some possible dates then I departed into the cold, slightly overcast but dry day.

Marcel was hovering with intent when I arrived at the members' bar. A slight movement of his head towards the doors leading to the members' viewing seats indicated he wanted to have a word. Marcel's idea of a word was to walk down the steps of the viewing seats, look over the safety barrier and safety net and nod towards the bookmakers' pitches at the end of the lawn. I followed his line of sight and initially did not see anything that caught my attention in the slightly dull light. I was just about to ask Marcel what he had seen when I saw Markham standing alone looking at the prices on Pauline's pitch. I hadn't seen him at first because he was very soberly dressed in a shirt, tie, dark shoes and trousers, and a country-style sports jacket. It was a good spot by Marcel.

"Thanks, Marcel. Syracuse, each way in the 3.50."

Marcel nodded then floated back up the steps into the members' bar.

I looked again at Markham. He placed a bet with Pauline then walked slowly across the lawn away from the pitches. The first race was still half an hour away, so I decided to speak to Pauline before a queue of punters formed. I walked out of the members' bar then along the internal gallery walkway to the escalators. I smiled to the bowler-hatted attendants then stepped onto the Down escalator and looked down. The only people on the adjacent, parallel, Up escalator were a man and woman who were standing together about halfway down. I glanced briefly at them then quickly looked at them again as they came towards me and materialised in my consciousness. It was Marty and Selena.

Selena saw me first and immediately released her hold on Marty's arm then stepped backward in an attempt to hide behind Marty. Marty looked behind at her puzzled and said something to her. She evidently replied because Marty quickly looked up, seeing me just as we drew level.

"Morning, Marty. Morning, Selena," I said cheerfully, as I continued downwards.

"Morning, James," replied Marty with a nervous chuckle as he and Selena continued upwards. Selena made a choking noise.

At the bottom of the escalator, I turned left to make my way to Pauline's pitch. I didn't look back up the escalators.

Pauline smiled when I approached. "Hello, James, that guy you asked me about last time is here."

"Hello, Pauline. Yes, I've seen him, although I hardly recognised him given how he's dressed."

"I nearly didn't recognise him either. Also, James, he normally has a confident, slightly smug demeanour, but today he seemed pre-occupied, even slightly deflated."

"Thanks, Pauline, I'll keep an eye out for him. You are a star." I gave her my bets for the first race.

"See you soon, James."

"Hopefully," I said.

Pauline smiled and turned to the next customer.

I walked back into the stand and went up the escalator to the King Edward VII level, but instead of turning to the members' bar, I went to the other side of the stand and looked down at the parade ring. None of the horses had yet entered for the first race. I scanned the wide walkways that bounded the parade ring, and to my surprise, I saw Marty and Selena heading towards the external gates. Selena had her head bowed and was walking slowly but determinedly. Marty was walking beside her, and his arm gestures suggested he was engaged in gentle pleading. Selena stopped, turned to him and shook her head. They then continued to the gates together and left the racecourse.

I stayed where I was and watched the horses come into the

parade ring, but I didn't really look at them. I was deep in thought. When the horses left the parade ring, I walked round to the other side of the stand to watch the first race. As usual, I avoided the members' viewing seats, which were generally very sparsely populated, and I sat in the seats occupied by racegoers who had purchased King Edward VII day tickets. These seats were almost completely occupied, but I found an empty one right at the front next to the safety barrier, and I sat there enjoying the atmosphere.

The race started, and the horse that I had bet at 10/1 each way was a neck second to the hot favourite. I decided to stay in my seat and check my analysis for the next race whilst everyone else crowded onto the steps then retreated into the stand to warm up. After five minutes of poring over the *Racing Post*, I thought I was satisfied with my choice of the two horses I was going to bet on each way in the next race. I then wondered whether the cold that was seeping into my body was causing me to jump to a conclusion in order to provide myself an excuse to go into the stand. Therefore, I decided to do so but once inside to look again at my analysis.

I stood up and turned towards the nearest steps. Someone was walking from the steps towards me, and he didn't look deflated. It was Markham, and he was moving with menace. I involuntarily glanced to the top of the steps, my escape route, and saw Marcel standing there looking at Markham. "You're being watched," I said, as Markham approached within a couple of metres, and I briefly looked again at Marcel.

At first, I thought Markham hadn't heard me as he continued walking but he stopped about a metre from me and turned to look to the top of the steps where Marcel was staring back steadfastly. Markham turned again to face me with pure malice on his face.

"I should throw you over there you interfering c..." he said, swivelling his eyes towards the safety barrier and safety net.

"That won't look good alongside the fraud charges."

I almost regretted saying that as I saw Markham twitch with almost uncontrollable hatred as the logical and instinctive parts of his brain battled as to whether to lash out. The logical part won, just, and I allowed myself another glance at the top of the steps where Marcel remained watching.

"You haven't got a hope of winning a fraud case against me. Your star witness is a dead parrot." Markham sneered.

"If the parrot isn't dead and is hidden somewhere, you should listen to what it says about you. It's not very complimentary."

Markham hesitated, which made me think that the parrot wasn't dead and that Markham hadn't listened to it.

"I'm not interested in what an effing parrot's got to say."

"So, it is still alive then?"

"I told you. I'm not interested in the f...... parrot," Markham said, raising his voice. He was again on the cusp of exploding.

"Why didn't you just postpone the Dagenham Glass fire when you got stuck in Truro? I only latched on to you because Jane said you were in Truro, and I wondered how you could have got to the Dagenham Glass fire in time to get the case. It never seemed plausible." A near certain way of defusing a situation is to give your protagonist something to think about. It worked.

"It was all set up, so I didn't want to postpone it, and even if she said I was in Truro and Jacobs were instructed on Dagenham Glass, I didn't think anyone would make anything of it. It was the only mistake I made," said Markham.

It wasn't, I thought, but I decided not to tell him of the others.

"I'll deny saying this to you, and your friend couldn't have heard it," Markham continued, nodding towards Marcel. Markham was beginning to feel confident.

"We both know that any case against you would need more than the evidence of a disputed conversation that hasn't been heard by a third party," I said, reducing the tension further.

Markham visibly calmed and tilted his head up slightly, the classic sign of someone who thinks they have gained a victory. He then turned around, walked to the steps and went up past Marcel into the stand.

After he entered the stand, I followed his route and stopped next to Marcel. "Thanks, Marcel," I said.

"I was in the members' bar when I saw him walk past and follow you into the day seats, so I came out of the bar and followed him. He spent the entire race at the top of the steps staring at you. I didn't like the look on his face, so after the race finished, I stayed watching him. He waited for everyone else to come up the steps and into the stand, then he went down the steps and made his way towards you. I was just about to shout out when you saw him, glanced at me and he stopped," said Marcel, which for him was quite a speech.

"You saved me," I said and patted his shoulder.

Marcel, returning swiftly to his modus operandi, nodded silently and went back into the members' bar. Syracuse won the 3.50.

Jemima said, "Selena was badly shaken when you saw her and Marty together and said 'morning' to her and Marty. Previously, they could have just about denied they were having an affair and might even have said that you were mistaken concerning what you saw at various times in Marty's office. Now she knows that you will tell everyone you saw them together at

Ascot, and she is worried about the consequences – so worried that she couldn't continue at Ascot despite Marty's pleading. She probably couldn't face the risk of running into you again. What are you going to do?"

"Tell everyone I saw them at the races together."

"Why?"

"Marty and Selena expect me to, and I'm not going to be party to covering up their affair by silence. Besides, it will give the other partners an opportunity to decide what to do about it. Previously, I think they've avoided doing anything because they don't think it interferes with the business, but I know it strongly affects how Marty conducts himself."

"They still might not do anything. They might say that them being seen together at Ascot doesn't affect the business."

"If I asked Selena on Monday if she enjoyed her day at the races, that would affect the business."

"James, you can't do that!" Jemima hissed.

"I can but I won't. I will tell the other partners, which should deal with those who are in denial about the affair. Thereafter, we'll see what happens."

"Markham's attire and the bookmaker's description of his demeanour obviously shows he was in defensive mode, but when he saw you, he flipped to attack."

"I think when Markham is angry, he can barely control himself."

"Do you think Markham would really have thrown you over the safety barrier?"

"I think he was very close to doing so, and Marcel's presence just say stopped him."

"You have almost certainly lost Markham a lot of money on those cases because insurers should win any civil case that the insureds might bring against them, if they even try. All of those insureds will probably end up in a criminal court and possibly in jail."

"They could probably help themselves a lot if they assisted the police with Markham, but so far they haven't."

"You didn't have your Dictaphone with you when you spoke to Markham today?"

"No."

"But you did when you visited Mr Pike's house to collect the keys for the Burtons' premises, and your recording of what the parrot said is crystal clear. It shows Mr Pike was lying when he said the parrot didn't say Markham's name, and it is strong evidence that Mr Pike at least, knew Markham before the fire. Taken with the shot parakeet, I think it is enough to implicate Markham in conspiring to start the Burtons' fire. Then there is the telephone call evidence on the Dagenham Glass fire. Taking that with the Ascot photograph and the Burtons' evidence, there is probably enough for the Crown Prosecution Service to run a case against Markham. Mind you, it will make British criminal history when your recording is played in court."

"Call the dead parrot!"